KARMA BURNS

Alexis Brown

Acknowledgements

First and foremost I have to thank God for blessing me with this wonderful talent and love of writing. Had it not been for Him, I would have never had the strength or confidence to complete this first novel!

Secondly to my beautiful mother, Ms. Vi: thank you so much for staying after me to be tenacious in this industry. It is your lesson of independence that will keep me moving forward in this!!

To my two beautiful children Star and Robert: thank you for being patient with me when all of my time was focused on completing this project. I love you both more than life itself and know that mommy will keep grinding in order to provide a better life for you!

Lastly, but definitely the mostest ☺ To my Best Friend, soul mate and confidante Mr. Brown: I am so glad that God made you just for me. You have been such a wonderful support system and husband to me throughout this whole process. You didn't give me too much flack on those nights that I was up until 5 or 6 AM because Karma Burns thoughts wouldn't allow me to sleep until they were down on paper. There is no way I would have made it without your motivation!! Smooches!

Cover Design: IZiggy Promotions, LLC

Editing & Publishing: April Rose Promotions

There are many others who have been encouraging in this quest (too many to name). You know who you are. Thank you very much!

Follow me on Social Media for special promotions, new releases and updates.

FB: www.facebook.com/authoralexisbrown

IG: www.instagram.com/authoralexisbrown/

Twitter: www.twitter.com/authalexisbrown

Website: www.authoralexisbrown.wix.com/lexy

For Bookings: aprilrosepromotions@gmail.com

Table of Contents

CHAPTER 1

Shauntel checked herself in the visor mirror of her 2012 Range Rover. The mirror light was the only thing shining in the dark night. She flipped her long black bang out of her eye, smiled at herself, applied her lipstick and blew a kiss at the mirror. A car door slammed jarring her out of her self-indulgence. She frantically looked around, spotting where the noise had come from. She was relieved. It was an older couple across the street. The man was helping what looked like his wife out of the passenger seat. Shauntel exhaled loudly and told herself she was just being paranoid. She closed the mirror and opened the truck door. Her Jimmy Choo's hit the concrete. Taking one last nervous look around to satisfy herself that no one had followed her, she quickly sashayed up to the condo door and used the key that Nate had recently given her and let herself in.

She stepped into the oversized living room that was appropriately decorated perfectly for a bachelor. It had monstrous sized ceilings and floor to ceiling windows. The colors were blacks, whites and grays with one red accented wall that made the room pop. Once inside the house, she removed her shoes and went into the master bedroom enjoying the view of the Detroit River. She heard what sounded like shower water and wasted no time disrobing and making her way into the master bathroom. She peeked in. "Oh Nate," she called out in her most sexy voice. Nate slid open the glass shower door smiling at her nakedness showing the deepest dimples ever made in skin so deep dark chocolate it would make any woman hungry. "Is there any room in there for me?" she asked with her hands on her voluptuous hips. He showed those pearly whites, "There is room for you anywhere I am." He stepped back so she could join him. As soon as she was inside, he slammed her against the shower wall and began to tongue her down! His hands were gently around her neck. She loved when Nate was aggressive with her. Her temperature rose to a level that she was sure was dangerous. Nate's rock hard erection was poking her in the right spot and that only made her hotter. Shauntel let out a loud moan and kissed him back hard. Not breaking their kiss, he spun her around so that the shower was hitting her back. He snatched her hair back so that her face was right under the water. He licked her neck in a circular motion and bit it. He trailed her neck and chest with his tongue stopping at her breast. With one breast in his hand, he licked her other already hardened nipple. He went to work on her tits sucking and licking like a crazed maniac. Shauntel got a firm grip on his member and stroked it up and down. He grabbed the back of her head and brought her face to his, licked her ear and whispered, "I was just getting out. Why don't we go to the bedroom, I've got something to show you." She obliged and they took their dripping wet bodies into the bedroom.

Nate shoved her down on the edge of the bed, snatched her legs open and knelt down on his knees. He placed his face right between her legs. His nose rested on her clit and his lips barely touched her LIPS! She could feel the heat from his breath. When he teased her like this she loved it and hated it all at once. She lifted her hips, let out a deep moan and begged, "Eat it baby." Nate shook his head no.

She whined, "Please!"

"Not yet," he whispered into her vagina taking a long whiff. Shauntel couldn't take it anymore. She grabbed his head and shoved his mouth into her mound grinding on his face. He sucked her clit and immediately she was cumming. In the middle of her ecstasy, there was a loud banging on the door. Shauntel froze. But she could tell Nate wasn't going to stop. "Nate, are you expecting somebody?" He kept going. "Nate!" He looked up at her with a devilish smirk, "Relax ma, they are going to have to come back later." "No Nate. You have got to see who it is." He got up reluctantly and started to get dressed. Shauntel was petrified.

Shauntel had been being stalked for the last month. But the worst of it was that she had no idea who the stalker was. Shauntel had not had an easy life by any means. Her father used to tease her all the time about being sticks and bones when she was little girl. Since all she longed for was her dad's approval, she started eating everything that wouldn't eat her. Her attempts paid off and she began to develop a thick shape. Unfortunately that only gave her dad more reason to insult her. Good year blimp, Mrs. Claus, and Fatty Watty were some of the nicer names her dad called her. She was only a size 10. But by this time, at age 13, Shauntel had already developed an unhealthy relationship with food. That year her father left her mother without one word. Despite numerous attempts to find him, her mom was unsuccessful. Her mother went into a deep depression that ended her up doing many long stretches at a mental institution. So her grandmother stepped in and raised her. Shauntel caught hell at school because she was bigger than all her classmates.

Her self-esteem took a whopping dive, as if it could get any lower. Shauntel was always a pretty girl and had straight black hair that hung halfway down her back. It was the only good thing her daddy had given her. He was light skinned, fine and had good hair. She had a striking resemblance to Tatyana Ali; only she was much prettier than Tatyana. By the time Shauntel graduated, she was a size 16 and never expected any man to want her because of her size. That is until she met Mike, who was almost 30-years her senior

Mike loved thick woman and he was filthy rich. Shauntel was curvy, but all those curves were in the right place! She had nice perky breasts that weren't too big, flat tummy, shapely hips and a firm round butt. Those were just compliments to her perfectly smooth cocoa colored skin and almond shaped eyes.

He showed Shauntel a life that until then she had only dreamed of. He bought her all kinds of expensive things, took her on all kinds of expensive trips, and introduced her to sex. As sick and twisted as it felt, Mike was like the daddy she never had. But he wasn't her daddy. He was her "DADDY"! He taught her street smarts, how to screw a man's brains out and how to make her own bread. But the one lesson he taught her that was priceless was that many men loved women her size so they would give her everything she demanded. Every since she met Mike, Shauntel had been working men out of their money. She had a beautiful mini mansion in Indian Village, a Range Rover, a Cadillac Escalade, a vacation home up north and a $750,000 bank account to show for it. Not to mention her designer clothes, accessories, furs & diamonds.

About a year ago, Shauntel was at the club with her girls when a guy sent her a drink. She scoped him out and decided he wasn't her type and sent him a drink back. The last thing she needed was some guy hovering over her all night because he bought her one drink. Some guys didn't get that all thick girls weren't desperate. The guy waited until the end of the night to approach her. He walked up extended his hand and introduced himself, "Hi my name is Nate." Uninterested she responded, "Hey Nate."

"How about you give me your number and I give you a call tomorrow?"

"Let's not and say we did," she said turning her back to him. He walked around to her face and gave her a piercing stare. It felt like he was peering into her soul. He smiled and simply said, "Ok, your lost," and walked away. Nate had her moist just from his smile. Nate was the complete opposite of her type. He was chocolate (strike 1) what could two chocolate people do together; he was average height (strike 2); and from his outfit he appeared to be middle class (strike 3).

However, she couldn't shake the feeling that he gave her when he stared at her. So before she left, she handed him a business card with her name and phone number on it. She figured with a frame like his, Nate would be a great bed partner. At the time Shauntel was dating four big ballers, a police officer and a city official and was happy with her life. She made it her business not to end up like her mom. So she let all her sugar daddies know that she was dating other people and never intended to be exclusive with any of them. She made each one wait at least 90 days before getting the goods (if they even got them). By then they were so desperate to get it that they were hooked when they finally did.

From the first day Nate called her, they talked on the phone for hours about everything and nothing. As hard as it was, she made Nate wait a whole 6 months before giving him any. But when they finally did it, it was so explosive! He had to be her soul mate. Three months later, Nate got on one knee and asked her to marry him, to cut off the other guys and be exclusively his. That was two weeks ago. She told Nate she had to think about it.

Shauntel had already made up her mind to marry Nate and subsequently had cut off all her other men friends. But she had to string Nate along for a minute like Mike had taught her to so that he would appreciate her. The only snag in her plans was that one of her ex-friends had turned stalker over the past month. She had replaced two sets of car tires, had her home broken into and trashed and received 5 life threatening letters. How had it come to this? The clicking of Nate's 357 Magnum broke her from her trance. He looked at her intently and said, "Stay here Mama, I'll be right back." She paced the floor hoping and praying that her stalker wasn't at the door and if he was that he wouldn't harm Nate.

Nate was taking an awful long time to come back and Shauntel was trying to follow his orders to stay in the bedroom but she was really getting worried. She picked up her Dolce & Gabana wrap dress, put it back on, and started towards the bedroom door. She heard what sounded like a struggle coming from the front of the house. She left the master bedroom and slowly walked down the hallway that led to the living room. Carefully peeking around the wall, she was shocked at what she saw.

Nate was having a fit! He had punched a hole in the wall and was throwing things around. When a lamp went flying past Shauntel's head after she ducked, Nate instantly stopped. He looked at her realizing he could have really hurt her. He walked quickly towards her and embraced her, "I'm sorry"

"Nate, what the hell is wrong with you?"

"It was that damn stalker. I tried to chase him but he got away." Nate walked to the front door and picked up a stuffed doll and held it up for her to see. It had a picture of Shauntel covering its face. The throat was slit. There was a sharp object through its chest and the whole bottom half of it was badly burned. Shauntel gasped. "This was stuck to the door. I swear if I catch that mofo I'm going to kill him!" Nate growled.

Shauntel shook her head at him. "Nate I think I'm going to get a restraining order."

"How are you going to do that when you don't even know who's doing this?"

"I've got a pretty good idea who it is. I told you about Byron." One of Shauntel's ex-friends with benefits, Byron had stalker written all over him.

"Shauntel that's not enough to get a judge to grant you a restraining order. Plus, I'm all the restraining order you need! What you're going to do is stay here with me and tomorrow you're going to apply for a CCW License. Until you get it I want you to keep one of my guns on you."

"Nate you know how much I hate guns."

"Baby I know but I'm not going to have you out here unprotected. You know you can just pack your things and move in here," Nate said with a smirk.

"I already told you Nate, I'm not shacking. We will have plenty of time to live together after we're married." Shauntel didn't realize that she'd let that slip until Nate's eyes lit up and he exclaimed, "So that's a yes?"

Tears of joy rolled down her face uncontrollably. She shook her head yes. He hugged her extra tight and planted kisses all over her.

"Thank you, baby. Thank you for deciding to be my wife!"

She had not meant to let it slip, but she was glad she had. She had kept Nate waiting long enough. "Tel, at least stay over here tonight so we can celebrate our engagement. I would feel much better knowing for sure that you're safe."

Shauntel had to admit that she was a little spooked and didn't want to be alone. But she had no idea how spooked she was going to be once she made it home. They got situated in his SUV. He felt in his pockets like he was looking for something. He told Shauntel, "Babe I'll be right back. I forgot something."

"Okay. I can call Tasha to tell her to meet me here in the morning for breakfast instead of at my place."

Nate went back in the house to retrieve what he had left and Shauntel called Tasha to tell her where she would be in the morning. She also let her best friend in on how she had accepted Nate's proposal. The two went back to elementary school. Tasha didn't have any siblings and her father was non-existent. To make matters worse, her mother was a combo addict. She did blow, crack, heroine and just about anything else that would get her high. So Tasha had to fend for herself most of her childhood until she met Shauntel and they instantly clicked. Not long after they met, Shauntel's grandmother had taken Tasha in like she was her own. That was why Tasha looked at Shauntel more like a sister than just her best friend. Tasha's mother sadly died of an overdose when Tasha was only 15 years old. Shauntel and her grandmother were there with her every step of the way when she was faced with the unimaginable responsibility of planning a funeral for the only blood relative she had really ever known.

The two talked almost the whole way to Shauntel's house about everything and nothing. Shauntel noticed that Nate wanted her attention so she finally disconnected the call from Tasha. *"Okay Tasha. I'll see you in the morning and please don't be late!"*

Nate pulled the truck over just about a mile from Shauntel's house. He walked around to her side of the car and opened the passenger door and knelt down at the curb facing her. "Shauntel Barnes, I never knew what people meant about meeting their soul-mate until the day I met you. You are more than my soul-mate. You are my best friend, the better half of me. You are my Eve but even better than that and I would rather die than to not have you by my side until the day that I do die. Would you make me the happiest man in the world and be my wife?" Shauntel couldn't believe that he was being so romantic. She cried and shook her head. "Yes.... Yes, we will be Mr. and Mrs. Whittington forever."

He stood up and they embraced. He took her face into both of his hands and kissed her affectionately. He reached in his pocket and pulled out the ring box and gently placed the beautiful princess cut quad diamond and platinum engagement ring on her finger.

She was extremely impressed; the ring was absolutely gorgeous. He had outdone himself.

Nate was going on and on about their wedding and marriage as he drove to Shauntel's house. Shauntel was pretending to be listening but had tuned him out and was in deep thought. This had to be karma. Shauntel's Grandma had explained karma to her at a young age. *"Baby, the Good Lord says you reap what you sow "No matter how long it takes everything you do, good or bad, will be done to you."* She knew that she hadn't been an angel but she felt that she hadn't been bad enough to deserve this stalking situation. She made a mental note to have that conversation with God later. "Shauntel, are you listening to me?" She chimed in on the tail end of what he was saying, "Yeah baby, I can't wait to be Mrs. Whittington either." She was mesmerized by the shimmer of the engagement ring on her finger. She playfully twisted it back and forth when it looked like she saw a reflection of fire in the diamond. "Damn!" Nate yelled. Shauntel's beautiful house was burning like hell!

Shauntel stumbled out of the car and onto the grass. The last thing she heard before losing consciousness was the sound of fire truck sirens.

Shauntel woke up 3 hours later. She had to blink her eyes repeatedly until she realized she was in an emergency room at Henry Ford Hospital. Nate heard her stirring and rushed over to her. He brushed her hair back with his hand, "You ok Mama?"

"I think so. What am I doing in here?" Before Nate could answer, the Doctor walked in. He looked like he was straight from Africa but when he spoke there was no doubt that he was from the islands.

"Ms. Barnes?"

"Yeah that's me," Shauntel responded with a frown. She hated hospitals.

"I'm Dr. Judkins, the resident for the night. Your test results are in."

Shauntel stared at the man with lifted eyebrows. After what seemed like an eternity, Dr. Judkins finally spoke. . . . . "Ms. Barnes, all of your test results are in and everything looks fine. I'm going to need for you to get some rest over the next few days and avoid stress at all costs. In your condition it is very easy for stressful situations to cause you to lose consciousness."

Shauntel looked at him bewildered, "My condition?"

"Yes," he said flatly, "You're eight weeks pregnant".

Before Shauntel or Nate could respond, a nurse peeked in the room and announced, "Ms. Barnes the police are here to speak with you".

The Dr. excused himself but let Shauntel know he would be back shortly. The two officers entered the room. It was a pudgy white man and a petite black lady who looked half his age. The pudgy man extended his hand as he told her, "I'm Officer Durham and this is my partner Officer Thornton." The lady cop nodded. Officer Durham looked at Nate, "If you don't mind excusing us for a moment."

"He's my fiancé; he can stay," Shauntel told the officer.

"Fine, Ms. Barnes where were you at the time of the fire at your home?"

"I was with my fiancé at his house. He took me home to get some things to stay overnight and when we got there..." She paused to hold back her tears and to regain her voice. She continued barely audible, "My house was on fire."

"Well did you leave anyone in the home?"

Shauntel frowned. "No. What is with these questions?"

"Does anyone else have a key, Ms. Barnes?"

"Look, either you tell me what is going on or I'm not answering another question!"

Nate rubbed his wife-to-be's arm, "Calm down, the doctor just told you that you're stressed. Look, officers you need to cough it up so she can get some rest!"

Officer Thornton interrupted, "Ms. Barnes, the investigation into the fire at your house shows suspicion of arson. Of course we can't say with any certainty right now, but there was no sign of a forced entry and we're sure that the fire was started from the inside."

Shauntel was confused. "What . . . . . How . . . . . ?"

"That's what we are working to find out Ms. Barnes and I can assure you that we will find out."

Shauntel wasn't sure but that last comment sounded like a threat.

"That will be all for now. If you think of anything, give us a call. We'll be in touch." Officer Thornton concluded handing her a business card. Shauntel was really spooked now because Nate was the only one with keys to her place but he was with her when the fire started.

Equipped with prenatal vitamins and instructions to take it easy until she saw her primary care doctor,

Shauntel was wheeled out of Henry Ford to Nate's car. The ride home was accompanied by an awkward silence that screamed, "What is she thinking? What is he thinking?" Finally Nate broke the silence. Rubbing Shauntel's thigh at a red light, "I don't know what is going on Tel, but I promise you everything's going to be alright." She responded with a partial smile and a nod. Nate knew about Shauntel's past. He trusted everything she'd told him. However, he was having a hard time dealing with the fact that his future wife was carrying a baby that might not be his. The next morning Nate and Shauntel lay comfortably in each other's arms. Once again they were awakened to banging on the door that sounded like the law. The only difference was that this time it was the law!

"Is Shauntel Barnes here?"

Nate peered at the officer with irritated anger, "Why the fuck yawl banging on my door this early?"

The big burly officer shoved his way in warning Nate, "We know she's here and if you don't want to go down for harboring I suggest you back the fuck up! Now where is she?"

Shauntel appeared in the living room, "What is going on?"

The officer's Hispanic partner picked up the conversation, "Ms. Barnes we have a warrant for your arrest."

"What!" Shauntel's chocolate skin turned beet red.

Nate yelled, "Warrant for what?"

"Arson, fraud, criminal mischief - take your pick. Either way you're coming with us." The officer let Shauntel get dressed before they handcuffed her and carted her off to jail. Nate felt really bad. He had to find a way to get Shauntel out of this mess since after all this was entirely his fault. If he hadn't felt that he needed to pressure Shauntel into being exclusive with him, she would not be going through this.

The officers treated Shauntel like a common criminal. She was in handcuffs until she was inside the police station, which looked like what she imagined Fort Knox would look like. Once inside, the big burly arresting officer took Shauntel's mug shots, fingerprints and shoe strings. Then he led her to her cell that was furnished with a toilet and a concrete block topped with a thin one-inch pad to sleep on. Shauntel had to will herself not to cry. If ever there was a time she needed to be strong it was now. She'd never even seen the inside of a jail until now. Since she'd left the house she had not spoken one word. Another lesson learned from Mike, "*Never talk to the police, they're worst than strangers.*" Thinking of Mike, Shauntel decided that was who she wanted to talk to whenever she got her one phone call. She knew he could get her out of this mess.

Shauntel had finally been able to calm her nerves enough to doze off, when she heard her cell door slam open, "Barnes, it's time to see the judge."

Shauntel rubbed her eyes in an attempt to wake up, "What time is it?"

"It's twelve o'clock Ms. Barnes." You're going before the judge at one."

Shauntel sat up, "But I haven't even made my phone call yet."

The officer gave Shauntel an uninterested look, "Not my problem!" She snatched Shauntel up, "Let's go!"

Shauntel and two other female prisoners were escorted across a skywalk from the jail to the courthouse. They were placed in a holding cell and told to keep quiet. The room smelled of urine, funk and something else Shauntel couldn't identify. She had to hurry up and get out of jail!

After what felt like an eternity, it was finally Shauntel's turn to see the judge. Her stomach was in knots and it felt like she was going to puke at any second.

"Case number 234514 the people of the State of Michigan versus Shauntel Miller on the charges of arson, willfully and maliciously setting fire, criminal mischief, burning of a dwelling/house, property damage and insurance fraud."

The prosecuting and defense attorneys took turns stating their names and which side they represented. Then both attorneys and the judge engaged in legal jargon that Shauntel didn't understand. Finally the Mexican lady judge peered over her glasses at Shauntel, "How do you plead Ms. Barnes?"

Shauntel was dumbfounded. Wasn't her attorney supposed to talk to her before she saw the judge? She wondered where they got these incompetent state appointed lawyers.

"Ms. Barnes?"

"Uh..... Judge..... Your honor, I'm not guilty."

"Fine. The court enters the plea of not guilty. Preliminary hearing is set for March 1, 2016."

The prosecutor interrupted, "Your Honor, in regard to bail, we have proof that Ms. Barnes is financially able to flee. We ask that bail be set accordingly." The prosecutor handed the bailiff Shauntel's bank statement.

The defense attorney rebutted, "Your honor, all my clients family is right here in Michigan and she has no reason to flee."

The judged looked over Shauntel's bank statements. She took her glasses and gave the defense a look that spoke louder than words. "Bail is set at five hundred thousand dollars no ten percent." With that the judge banged her gavel.

CHAPTER 2

Meanwhile, Nate was multitasking. He was driving all over town, making phone calls and smoking blunt after blunt. He had to find his best friend Corey so that they could rectify this situation. Nate had never loved a woman like he loved Shauntel and there was nothing in the world he wouldn't do for her. He was determined to prove that once again today! He had been driving around for 3 hours now, checking every spot he thought he might find Corey. So far he'd called Corey's baby mama 5 times, his mom about 3 times, and left an uncountable number of voicemails on his cell phone. Nothing was panning out. Nate felt on the edge. Right before he snapped, his cell phone sang, Big Punisher's, "Off With His Head". Bingo! Nate snatched the phone open.

"Corey where the fuck you at man?"

"Dawg calm down."

"Nigga don't tell me to calm down. We need to meet right now on some real shit!"

"What is wrong Nate?"

"I'll explain when I see you. Meet me at Rouge Park in 15 minutes by the hill." Nate slammed the phone shut and punched the gas so hard that he burned rubber.

Though not huge, Nate had always been solidly built. As a kid, he beat the biggest of his peers. One time four boys tried to jump him and he beat all of them. He studied karate and boxing and even earned his Black Belt. He wanted so bad to be a professional boxer, but his adopted mother wasn't having it. She told him there was no way in the world that her only son was going to end up like Muhammad Ali. So at age 20, he got a job as a bouncer. When he realized how much money was in security, he began to save 50% of his pay and within a year he started his own private security company. He recruited most of his boys that he had worked in the industry with. Corey was one who had been working with him from day one.

A few of Nate's friends had made it in the entertainment industry. So they referred him to their Hollywood friends whenever they were in town. Because of that, Nate's business had become very successful. Stars out of town even specially requested his team sometimes. Nate wasn't filthy rich but despite Shauntel's initial assessment, he was more than middle class at his 30 years young.

Nate hadn't had an easy childhood by any means. When he was just a baby, his mother was a teenage single mother who was struggling financially. She had no family support and Nate's father had disappeared as soon as he found out she was pregnant. Her only resolve was to go to the welfare office to seek some assistance. They refused to help her. The staff had been so nasty to her over such a long period of time that she finally decided that she would prove a point to them by leaving her baby there for them to take care of him.

She had been waiting to see a welfare worker for over three hours. She was hungry and tired and something had snapped. She left Nate at the front desk and stormed out in hopes that the state would get the point that she really needed some assistance. Unfortunately, the state didn't get the point at all. Instead, they took Nate into foster care and despite her many attempts, his mother was never able to regain custody of him.

Over the next few years he was bounced from foster home to foster home. The things he had witnessed over those years were so unimaginable that he tried his best to suppress those thoughts. Finally at the age of 5, he was taken to a foster home of a husband and wife who absolutely loved kids. The Whittington's were a loving middle class family. Mrs. Whittington always wanted children but she didn't want to have to go through the diaper and bottle phase. So her and her husband decided they would adopt and help save some child's life who really needed it. Nate was that child. Mrs. Whittington would never forget the first day she met him. She peered into his eyes at the foster center and she saw nothing but good and pain. She knew with a little nurture and love that she could mold him into what God had intended for him to be. After two years of being Nate's foster parents, they decided to adopt him. They gave him their last name and they became his mom and dad. They were the only parents he ever knew.

He did search for his natural mother later on in life and when he found her she had explained the situation to him. She apologized over and over again and tried her best to make the best out of a situation gone wrong. They had since developed a decent enough relationship, but he would always consider Mrs. Whittington his real mother.

Nate pulled up to the hill at Rouge Park and spotted Corey's Lincoln Navigator. He pulled in behind him and parked.

Before Corey could close the car door, Nate was talking, "Yo dawg, I need to get at yo mans! This shit is getting out of hand!"

"I've been trying to find him since you told me about the fire." "Man we are wayyy beyond the fire. My girl is locked up."

"For what?"

"Arson. They think she set her own place on fire!"

"Damn this shit is already out of hand."

"That's what I'm trying to tell you. We have to find him and put an end to this."

"Nate, this nigga is good at what he does but he's even better at hiding. I'm telling you I've looked everywhere and you know I can usually find a nigga."

Nate chuckled. "Yeah, I know. I think we're going to have to call The Eye. If anybody can find him, he can."

"That's what's up. Let me check some traps and see what I can come up with and I'll holla in a couple of hours."

"Cool. If I don't answer leave a voicemail. I have to get downtown and check on my girl."

Nate sped down the Jeffries Freeway deep in thought about what he was going to do to save his wifey. He was oblivious to the fact that a State police car had been following him for the last two miles. As he merged onto the Fisher Freeway, the loud sirens behind him startled him. In his surprise, he dropped the blunt in his lap, but didn't realize it. He looked in his rearview mirror. "Fuck, not now!" He screamed. Then he felt the burn in his lap. He quickly snatched the blunt up and patted the fire out of his lap. He contemplated if he should pull over. He didn't need a ticket right now and even worse, he could not afford to go to jail for weed. He had to be free so he could get Shauntel out of jail. After thinking about his situation for a couple of minutes, he finally pulled over. He figured he would talk his way out of this somehow.

Nate snatched open his ringing phone as waited for the officer to approach.

"Yeah."

"If you don't want your bitch to be turned butch in prison, you know what you better do!" The line went dead. The person on the phone had been using voice-changing software and the number had shown private on the caller ID. So Nate had no idea who it was.

The officer stepped out of his patrol car and slowly approached the 2016 Jaguar XJ with his hand on his gun. When he reached the driver's door, he tapped on the window. Nate rolled down the window and the officer gave the normal spiel, "License and registration please". Nate reached over in the glove box frantically searching for the requested documents.

"You know why I pulled you over?"

The voice was familiar to Nate so he stopped looking for his registration and looked up out the window and realized it was Calvin, one of his High School classmates. *Nate must have really been distracted to have not noticed Calvin before. Calvin stood at a towering 6 foot 7 inches tall and weighed about 300 pounds. He also had vitiligo, a skin disease that causes the pigmentation of the skin to die giving its victims a distinguished appearance.*

"Yo, Nate, man I didn't know that was you."

In a defeated voice, Nate asked, "What's up Calvin".

"Nothing much, another day another dollar. Just out here trying to do my job. Man do you know how fast you were going?"

"Not really Calvin, I've got a serious emergency right now."

"I clocked you doing 90, but as I followed you for the last 3 miles you hit speeds as high as 100."

"My bad, but like I said, I've got a serious situation and I really need to go. Can't you just let me off with a warning or something?"

Nate knew that even though most people thought that Calvin was a big mean police officer, he was actually really cool and he hoped that would work in his favor right now. A little skeptical, Calvin asked, "What's the emergency?"

"My pregnant fiancé is in the county for something she did not do. I need to get down there and see if I am able to bail her out!"

"Man that's fucked up".

"So can you give me a break today?"

Calvin thought about it for a minute. "How about this, I'll write you a ticket, because the police commissioner is on our asses about meeting quota. Then when it's time to go to court, I will mysteriously not show up so that the judge will throw the ticket out. And to make up for the lost time of me writing the ticket, I'll be your escort to the county with my sirens on."

Nate exhaled, "Bet".

****

Nate pulled into the police officers' parking lot adjacent to the jail right behind Calvin. Calvin pulled over and had a short conversation with the parking lot attendant. Then the attendant waved Nate into a parking space, gave him a tap on the car hood and said "you're good buddy". Nate waved his hand at the attendant to show his appreciation. He walked over to Calvin's patrol car and told him, "Good looking out" while giving him some dap.

Calvin handed Nate his business card out of the window. "Give me a call if you need any help and I'll do what I can."

Nate quickly made his way up the steps into the jail. He hated being inside police stations and jails. There were too many of his people who called places like this home. He walked up to the information desk noticing the oversized officer having a phone conversation that did not seem to be work related at all. Nate took being ignored for all of thirty seconds, and then he knocked on the window, "Yo, bro". The officer's only response was to look at Nate like he was bothering him and to throw up his index finger, meaning wait a minute. Nate was getting impatient. He tried to remain calm but the obvious disrespect from the desk officer was making it really hard. Just when Nate was about to lose it, the officer laid the phone down and looked up and asked through the window, "can I help you?"

Nate told him he was there to find out if there was a bond for Shauntel.

"Spell her name."

Nate did. The officer typed the information into the computer and said to Nate, "I've got to call over to where she is to get some more information. Have a seat". Nate exhaled really loudly and did as he was told. He sat down but in his mind this was the end of the road for this officer. If he didn't give him some information right away, there was going to be a serious problem.

****

Robert Milliken, Shauntel's state appointed lawyer walked into the holding cell and motioned for her to come over to the side of the room with him. Once she was near him, he greeted her, "Ms. Barnes, I'm sorry that I wasn't able to speak to you before your arraignment but they threw your case on me at the last minute. You have a pretty good case because most of the evidence looks circumstantial at best. But keep in mind, depending on what develops in the prosecution's case; you may need to take a plea."

"And why the hell would I do that?"

"I'm not saying you should or shouldn't just yet. I'm just saying that might be an option later. I'm going to talk to the prosecutor and see what they're offering."

"I don't care what they're offering. I'm not pleading to shit! I'm innocent!"

"Ms. Barnes, you are charged with 5 felonies and there was no sign of forced entry into your home. The only fingerprints found in your place were yours. Not to mention you stand to receive a hefty amount of money from your insurance company. So you see, your case is not open and shut."

"Look Mr. Mil-li-ken, you do what you have to do, but I'm not pleading guilty to something I didn't do," Shauntel went back to her original seat leaving Robert Milliken standing in the corner alone.

As Shauntel was being escorted back to her cell, she saw her Cousin Erica's best friend Harmony. She was a guard at the jail. They locked eyes and Shauntel's desperation showed. She mouthed to Harmony from across the room, "*I need to talk to you.*" Keeping her cool Harmony nodded as to not tip anyone off that she was an acquaintance of the accused. Finally Shauntel was catching a break. About 10 minutes after Shauntel was back in her cell she heard the familiar high-pitched voice. "Shauntel, what are you doing in here?"

"Long story, I'll have to tell you that later. Right now I need your help."

"What's up?"

"They haven't given me my phone call yet. I need to call Mike so I can get the hell out of here."

"Ok, I'll see what I can do."

Even though Mike had a wife at home that he would never leave, he always had a special love for Shauntel. When she broke it off with him, he told her she could always call him if she needed anything. Shauntel didn't have time to try to figure out *if* Nate could get her out. She needed to get out ASAP! And the one person who she knew would deliver was Mike.

****

Shauntel was so happy to have Mike as a friend. He didn't hesitate to come and bond her out of jail. Once she was in the chauffer driven car with him, she gave him the rundown on all that had happened, including the fact that she was pissed off at Nate for not showing up to court and for not even trying to bail her out. She purposely left out the part about her being pregnant and engaged. She wasn't sure how Mike would swallow that pill. Mike listened intently like he always did before sharing his wise advice. After Shauntel was done venting, he chimed in.

"It sounds like there is some really thick shit going on and you need some time to just chill and collect your thoughts away from all outside influences. So, what I suggest is that you let me take you shopping since you lost everything in the fire. Then I will put you up in the Presidential suite at my Hotel. I will call up my other driver to stay there just in case you need to go anywhere and I will also have two of my guys to stay and watch out for you. While you're evaluating this situation, I will call my attorney so that he can get up to speed on the case."

Shauntel had zoned out right after he'd said her favorite words *"let me take you shopping"*. Mike was waiting on a response, but not getting one.

"Shauntel?"

"Huh?"

"Are you ok?"

"Yeah.....yeah, Mike I'm fine. It's just that you said my favorite words. You know how therapeutic shopping is for me. "

He chuckled. "Don't I know it?"

"Mike?" Shauntel said his name just above a whisper.

"Yeah."

"Thank you for being such a good friend and for always having my back and I'm going to pay you back the bond money as soon as I get situated."

"Don't worry about that right now. The most important thing is for you to get rested so that you can come out swinging hard and knock this case out and also the coward motherfucker pulling all of these antics."

They hit Somerset mall and as soon as Mike handed her his black card, Shauntel quickly got down to business. She was a professional shopper and she was not disappointed that day. She hit all her favorite stores Tiffany & Co., Louis Vuitton, Nine West, Niemen Marcus, Bath and Body Works, just to name a few. She bought five pairs of Designer Sunglasses, many purses and shoes, plenty of clothes from Nordstrom and Macy's, a laptop computer and a charger for her cell phone because her battery was dead. Then she hit the Nordstrom Spa and had an herbal rap, a facial, a pedicure, a manicure and a full body massage. Mike stayed in the Metro Car making and taking business calls for the whole four hours that she was shopping. She had so many bags that the Concierge had to wheel her stuff to the car for her. Shauntel made her way back to the car looking like a new woman. Mike asked her if she was hungry and she hadn't noticed she was until then with all that was going on. They went to *Benihana* and had a feast.

Mike owned a hotel chain called Iced that was exclusively for high-end clients. You had to be someone well known to stay there. You also had to be on the approved guest list to even make a reservation. The only way to get on that list was directly through Mike. There were strict privacy guidelines guests had to follow and they signed agreements to that effect. They all knew if they violated the guidelines, they would be facing a huge lawsuit.

The hotels were gated and purposely located in areas where normal people would never notice them for guests' privacy. The media suspected the hotels existed, but they had no proof because they couldn't past the gate to prove it and the hotel wasn't visible from the street.

In each hotel, Mike had a room built just for him and presidential suite was an understatement for it. They pulled up to the hotel valet and the valet manager was at the car door in five seconds flat. He opened the door for Shauntel while the concierge was loading all of her bags onto the cart. Her and Mike took the elevator up to the 30th floor and walked to the door of Mike's suite at the same time the concierge did. When Shauntel opened the door the smell of oriental lilies sweetly enveloped her nostrils. They were her favorite flowers. Mike was such a great guy, too bad he was taken. She stepped onto the white marble floors of the 5-bedroom suite with 50-foot ceilings, gold pillars and marble floors to see so many bouquets of flowers that she could not count.

"Oh Mike, what would I do without you? You are the best friend I could ever ask for. You know you have to stop spoiling me like this, nobody is ever going to measure up to you."

"No one has to measure up Shauntel, as long as I have breath in my body, I will spoil you and even after that. You know that you are my heart and in another lifetime under other circumstances, you would be Mrs. Mike Bradford.

No words would be able to express her feelings, so Shauntel embraced him like he was her lifeline and he did the same. After they released each other, Mike announced, "Chef D is going to stay here as long as you're here. Just let him know the day before what you would like to eat for breakfast, lunch, dinner and snacks and he will make sure you have it. Now if you just feel the need to cook, I had the freezer, fridge and cabinets stocked as well. And of course there are plenty of bottles of your favorite Moscato in the fridge also. I'm going to go handle my business so that you can get settled in." With that, he gave Shauntel a friendly peck on the check and left with his routine way of saying bye, "Truth".

The Concierge was just about finished unloading all of Shauntel's shopping bags. She plugged her cell phone on the charger and powered it on. She grabbed a twenty dollar bill out of her purse to hand the Concierge and he shook his head no, "Mr. Bradford has already taken care of it, have a comfortable stay." He let himself out.

Shauntel's cell phone started to ring back to back with the notification of messages. She was too exhausted to deal with that right then so she went into the master bedroom and ran her a hot bubble bath in the Claw foot Jacuzzi Tub and turned the Bose theatre system to the Jazz station.

CHAPTER 3

"Visitor for Shauntel Barnes," the officer yelled. *'It's about time'*, Nate thought to himself. As he approached the information window, Nate noticed the bothered look still on the officer's face.

"May I help you," the officer asked again with the same attitude.

Nate was really getting impatient. "You just called me up here for Shauntel Barnes."

"Oh yeah, she was bonded out about 45 minutes ago."

"Bonded out? What the fuck?! You've had me sitting here all this time for nothing?"

"Not for nothing. To tell you she's gone."

"Whatever, man. Who posted bond for her?"

"I'm sorry sir that is privy information that I am not allowed to share with you."

"Privy?"

"That's right, private, secret, something you cannot know, and basically I'm not telling you."

"You'd better be glad that I cannot afford to be locked up today. You don't want to see me in the streets motherfucker."

"Sir, is that a threat?"

"Naw, that's a fact," Nate growled as he left the station.

The officer was giggling. He had accomplished his goal.

Nate sat in his car trying to collect his thoughts. He had already called Shauntel's cell phone 3 times with no answer. *"Where the hell could she be,"* he thought out loud. He picked up the cell phone one last time and called Tasha, Shauntel's best friend. Tasha snatched the phone open and said hello really loud attempting to talk over the loud background music. Nate yelled, "Tasha".

"Hold on I can't hear you let me turn this music down." The volume of the music went down. "Hello."

"Tasha this is Nate, have you talked to Shauntel."

Tasha exhaled, "No I haven't. Something has to be wrong if you're calling me. What's going on Nate?"

"It's some deep shit that I really can't get into right now, but it is important that I find her A-S-A-P. So if she calls you please tell her to get in touch with me immediately."

"Hold on playa, how you calling my phone requesting favors and information when you are not willing to give up any?"

"Tasha, look she is okay. It's just a really long story that she will have to tell you later. Just do me this one favor. You know I wouldn't be asking you to if it wasn't extremely important!"

"Yeah, I know but you know that's my girl, more like my sister, so I have to look out for her. I called her earlier, but her cell phone was going straight to voicemail and I thought that was odd. That girl doesn't go anywhere without a phone charger. But I will keep my ear to the street and if I hear anything, I'll make sure to have her holla.

Just remember you owe me one and next time you call asking for info, be prepared to give up some."

"While you're talking about next time, next time turn that loud ass music down before you answer the phone."

"Whatever!"

"Thanks," was all Nate could muster up exhaustedly.

He ended the call and decided to go to his place in hopes that Shauntel would be there.

Nate entered the condo and threw his keys on the console table, "Shauntel". There was no response. He searched the whole place including the backyard and garage, but there was no sign of Shauntel. He called Shauntel one last time and left her a voicemail:

"Baby, I really need you to call me back. I'm worried about you. I went to the jail and they told me that you were already bonded out. I didn't expect you to go to court so soon so I was out here trying to figure out my rescue plan for you. I hope that everything is okay and that you are not mad at me. I really need to see and hold you to make sure you're okay. Call me as soon as you get this message, I love you."

With all his resources exhausted, Nate decided to go take a hot shower with hopes that Shauntel would be calling him back by the time he was finished.

1.

****

'What the hell is going on', Tasha thought to herself. She knew she would have to find Shauntel. She was a professional at getting ghost. No matter how hard she tried to hide though, Tasha always knew where to find her.

First Tasha called Shauntel's house phone and was even more worried now from the fast busy signal she got. Then she called Mike's presidential suite at the hotel in Detroit. There was no answer. Her third call was to the suite at the Iced Hotel in Troy and on the third ring, Shauntel answered the phone winded. "Hello?"

"Girl, are you okay?"

"Yeah,   what's   up   Tasha?" "I should be asking you what's up. Why are you out of breath?"

"I just got out of the tub so I had to run to the phone. How did you know where I was?"

"Think about who you're talking to. You know if anybody can find you, I can."

"True, Inspector Gadget," Shauntel answered with a chuckle.

"Okay, tell me what's going on. Why is Nate calling *me* looking for you?"

"It's a long story..."

Tasha cut her off, "Not that bullshit again, that's the same thing Nate said. Somebody better tell me something."

"Okay, okay, calm down. I went to jail..."

"You what?!!!!"

"I said calm down, now do you want to know or not?"

"Go ahead."

"Long story short, my house was burned down and from the excitement, I fainted. I woke up in the hospital, where I found out that I'm pregnant. After me and Nate made it home and fell asleep, the police came bright and early and arrested me saying that the fire at my house was suspicious and that I burned it down for the insurance money."

Tasha was silent.

"Tasha?"

"Yeah, I'm here. I'm just trying to process all that you just said. That's a lot of shit!"

"Who are you telling?"

"And, you're sure you're alright after all of that?"

"Not really, but if I keep saying it, maybe it will be true. I would be better if I could really talk this through."

"Okay you want me to come out there?"

"Nah, I'll have Mike's driver bring me to pick you up and then we will figure out somewhere to go talk. I need some air"

"Cool, Auntie Tasha will be ready."

"Girl, listen to you. I'll be there in an hour, Auntie."

They both laughed, hung up and prepared to get ready.

Shauntel was a stickler about being on time, that's why Tasha knew that Shauntel was really not alright when she showed up an hour and a half later looking bewildered. Her outfit hair and makeup were all on point as usual, but she had a dazed look in her eyes.

"What's up Chica," Tasha said with a smile while entering the car.

They embraced.

"Apparently you," Shauntel replied. "You're looking good as usual".

"You know how we do."

Tasha was an average size with a heavy top. She didn't have much backside, but what she was missing down bottom, she more than compensated for with her F cup breasts that sat up perky as ever. She carried her weight well in her Seven boot-cut skinny Jeans with a black shoulder slit tunic with a plunging neckline and black leather strappy 5-inch sandal heels. Likewise, Shauntel was dressed to impress with a pink silk wrap blouse that showed a hint of cleavage and her black fitted jeans trimmed in pink and her 6-inch pink floral mesh heels with the toe out. The only difference was that Shauntel had her clothes specially made by a lady name Dyana who was a designer for celebrities who took credit for her fashions but paid her heftily for her services.

"So where are we going Shauntel?"

"That's what I was going to ask you, with all that's going on, you are going to have to be the brains of the operation."

"You know I've got you. Are you hungry?"

"I don't have much of an appetite. I thought you were supposed to be hungry when you are pregnant."

"It's probably just all of the stress; you will be soon from what I've heard. What do you want to do?"

"I don't really know. I need to do something physical to get all of this frustration out!"

"Do you want me to call Nate then?"

"Ha ha, very funny."

"I'm just joking, my boy is a trainer at the boxing center, we could go over there and you could let off some steam there."

"That sounds perfect! Except, boxing in heels is not the vision."

"They have a sports shop there. We could buy some sneakers and fitness outfits."

"Cool."

Tasha told the driver where to go and Shauntel proceeded to give her the longer version of events from the past few days.

"So let me get this right, Nate did not come to court or to the jail to bail you out?"

"That's right, and I'm pissed off about it so I'm not talking to him right now. He left me a voicemail saying he was sorry and when he got there I was already gone. But sorry doesn't cut it in this situation. He should have been Johnny on the spot!"

"All he said was sorry?"

"No, some other *B-S* about he was out trying to get a rescue plan together."

"You know we go back like four flats on a Cadillac, and you know I'm going to keep it one hundred with you. Nate called *me* because he was worried about you. How rare is that? I think he was genuinely trying to work it out and from what you told me, they did process you out really fast. You know how slow those people at the county usually move. So maybe you should at least listen to what he has to say."

"You're right about how quick I was processed, but that's just it, I need a man who makes moves and has connections. Mike was there in 2 point 2 and I was out."

"I feel you Shauntel, but we both know that Nate is a good guy and he will do anything in the world for you, maybe just be a little patient and hear him out."

"Maybe later, but he is going to have to suffer for now."

Tasha felt really bad for all that Shauntel was going through. Especially, since she had recently gotten over some jealous feelings that she had been harboring for Shauntel for years. She wanted everything to work out for Shauntel and prayed that her past envy would not cause harm to anyone or to their friendship.

****

"Hello?"

"Hey Nate, I hit the lottery, The Eye will be on you in about two minutes."

"That's what's up. I'll get with you after I handle this business."

"Alright, holla if you need some assistance."

Two minutes later, Nate's phone rang, he looked at the caller ID and it read *000-000-0000*. He picked up the phone. "Talk to me."

"You looking for something?"

"You know it."

"Ok meet me at the Observatory in 3 hours."

"Alright."

Nate knew that 3 hours meant 30 minutes. So he grabbed his gun and keys and headed for the meeting place that The Eye used.

When Nate got there 15 minutes later, The Eye was already there watching him pulling up. Once The Eye was certain that Nate hadn't been followed, he appeared. The Eye was a small man with a Napoleon complex. He stood about 5'8" and weighed about 170lbs with bright skin, brush waves and a goatee. He was smooth and knew how to blend into a crowd. He was extremely resourceful and could find people even the FBI couldn't find. He also knew how to make people disappear. Nate told The Eye all about his problems and The Eye gave him a price and told him to give him 48 hours to track down the target.

****

Two days later, Nate crept up on the target and though he was startled the target was good at hiding his surprise, "Where's my money?" The mysterious looking slender guy asked Nate.

"You'll get it, but first I need you to listen to me real good." Nate annunciated well and slowly, "This is the last money I'm giving you and you are going to leave town within 24 hours. Unless you want to catch some hot shit!"

"Are you threatening me?"

Nate ignored the question, popped his trunk, pulled out the brown paper bag and threw it at the man's feet, "Ten thousand".

"I told you twenty-five thousand."

"That's where you've got shit twisted. You don't tell me! Now, there's ten thousand, take it or leave it."

"How about I take it and make things much worse for you?"

Nate was on the guy with his Glock pointed in his jaw so fast that the guy didn't have time to prepare, "How about I just blow this shit-box you call a head off and everything will be great for everybody? I don't usually give second chances but since this is partially my fault, I'm offering you a break this time. But, this is a different kind of ball game. Two strikes and you're out! Trust, if you try me, it will be lights out! "

The guy was shaking and sweating profusely, "Alright, it's all good, you can put that heater away."

Nate shoved the gun into his face further, "You sure? Be real sure before you answer that because I can make you sure if not."

"Yes," the guy whispered.

Nate lowered the gun and shoved the guy on the ground, "That's what I thought".

Nate hopped in his car and peeled out. He picked up his phone and called The Eye. "You on it?"

"Like a fly on shit!"

"Cool, one false move, take that fool out."

"No doubt."

Nate went home and packed him an overnight bag. He knew that what he just did could be the end to his problems or it could be a war that he had to be prepared for. So until he knew which one it was, he needed to lay low. He called Shauntel and left another message.

"Tel I've figured out by now that you must be mad at me and I understand that. I was a little slow getting downtown and I apologize. This is very important though, we have a little situation right now and my place is not safe. So whatever you do, please don't go to my place. I really wish you would at least send me a text letting me know that you are okay so that I will at least be able to have some peace since I haven't had any since you were arrested. Remember baby, you're my everything and I love you."

He hit I-75 and proceeded to the hotel he always stayed at whenever he was providing security for celebrities, The Iced Hotel of Troy.

CHAPTER 4

Shauntel decided to have a girls' night at the room since most of her free time had been spent with Nate over the last month. She invited Tasha, her cousin Erica and Erica's best friend Harmony to the room for a sleepover. The girls were having a ball listening to old school hip-hop and R&B on the stereo, drinking Moscato and laughing about the latest gossip. Erica was one of the best hairdressers on the east coast and she always kept up with the latest hot topics. "Have yawl heard about the new sticky but pads that stick to your butt so that you don't have to worry about them falling off?"

Harmony snapped her head around. "The What?"

"Yeah, they're butt pads and they come in all different sizes, shapes and materials according to your preference." Erica loved being the newscaster.

Shauntel stood up and shook her hips, "I know I don't need any butt pads."

Erica looked around, "I know who does."

Everybody looked at Tasha and busted out in laughter.

"Screw you heffas, I might not have all that ba-dunk-a-dunk, but '*got milk*' Be-atches?" Tasha squeezed her breasts.

They all fell out laughing.

Harmony chimed in, "Girl that's enough milk to shutdown a thousand farms."

Tasha gave Harmony the finger.

Erica had to know, "Tell the truth Tasha, are those things real?"

"Is that hair real?"

"Now you know."

"Thought so."

They continued on throughout the evening with all of their chatter and jokes. Shauntel slipped into the master bedroom to check her messages. She heard the message Nate had left earlier:

"Tel I've figured out by now that you must be mad at me and I understand that. I was a little slow getting downtown and I apologize. This is very important though, we have a little situation right now and my place is not safe. So whatever you do, please don't go to my place. I really wish you would at least send me a text letting me know that you are okay so that I will at least be able to get some peace

since I haven't had any since you were arrested. Remember baby, you're my everything and I love you."

She listened to the rest of his messages and started feeling really bad about ignoring him for so long. He sounded really stressed and he mentioned not going to his place. Now she was starting to worry about him. She sent him a text message that simply read *'I'm ok'.* He quickly responded *'thanks for letting me know, I miss holding you, but I'm patient, good night'.*

Shauntel made a mental note to make sure she called him the next day right after her meeting with the attorney Mike hired for her.

****

Shauntel woke up the next afternoon and realized she had overslept. It was one O'clock in the afternoon and the attorney was scheduled to be there at two O'clock. The baby had been making her sleep like that of a hibernating bear's. She jumped up and ran to the bathroom to quickly take a shower and try to get herself together. She hopped out, lotioned her body, brushed her hair up into a hair clip, and threw on her orange sundress and matching orange Jimmy Choo

Sandal heels. She threw on some gold Mac lip-gloss, laid out some light snacks and had ten minutes to spare. The attorney showed up 5 minutes early and that was a plus for him because tardiness was her biggest pet peeve. Shauntel opened the door and the attorney extended his hand, "Ms. Barnes?"

Shauntel shook his hand, "Yes, but you can call me Shauntel."

"Ok, Shauntel, I'm Attorney Jackson Hartford."

"Nice to meet you, please come in."

Jackson Hartford had an air of confidence. He was a tall man at least 6 feet 3 inches and he was slender with smooth caramel skin. He wore a gray stuffy suit with a white and gray stripped shirt, a black tie and black leather loafers. His glasses looked to be from the last decade. He was not bad looking, just too stuffy and unfashionable. Shauntel wanted to give him a makeover and thought to herself *'maybe then he would find a wife'* as she noticed he wasn't wearing a wedding ring.

They sat down at the dining table. Shauntel was playing with her hair the way she always did when she had feelings of anxiety. Mr. Hartford quickly said, "Let's get down to business."

"Shauntel I have reviewed your case and I see there are a lot of charges. The good and bad news is that most of the evidence is circumstantial. Because it is circumstantial, I will need to ask you some questions so that we can have a fool proof game plan when we go to court for your evidentiary hearing. Before I do, I just want you to know that I am real familiar with the District Attorney on your case and he is known for bringing trumped up charges. It's a strategy he uses to try to convince people to take a plea to a lesser charge later in the case. I can assure you that we will not be pleading to anything unless there is no other option and with me there is always another option!"

"That sounds more like it Mr. Hartford, that court appointed attorney was talking out of the left side of his mouth."

"Trust me. I will be with you every step of the way. Now, let me set a precedent for our relationship, I need you to be completely honest with me at all times and I will do the same. Everything you tell me is confidential under the attorney-client privilege law. Buckle up, here we go......". Mr. Hartford got his pen and pad ready.

"Have you ever been to jail for anything other than this arrest?"

"No."

"Juvenile court records are sealed. Do you have any juvenile court records?"

"No."

"Any traffic tickets or misdemeanors?"

"I got a speeding ticket three years ago."

"And what was the outcome of that?"

"The stupid cop lied and said I was doing 15 miles over the speed limit and the even stupider judge believed him so I had to pay a $500 fine and got 2 points on my license. They have fallen off."

"Does anyone else have a key to your home?"

Shauntel hesitated. She did not want to get Nate into trouble because she knew he would never to do anything like burn her house down. She decided to be honest. "Yes".

"Who?"

"My fiancé."

"What is his name?"

"Nathaniel Whittington."

"Does he have a criminal record?"

"With all due respect Mr. Hartford, I don't think that is relevant."

He gave her an exhausted look. "Shauntel, my job is to win your case and keep you out of jail. Therefore, everything is relevant," he said flatly.

"Yes, he went to jail for assault a few years ago. He was a bouncer and there was an unruly customer who he had to.... let's say restrain."

"What was the outcome of that?"

"He pled guilty to avoid having to keep going back to court and missing work."

2.

"What was his sentence?"

A year probation."

"Did he ever violate probation?"

"I don't think so."

"You're not sure?"

"No, I didn't know him then. But, I think his record is clear since he was able to get a license to carry a concealed weapon."

"Ok, now to make sure that my information is accurate, how much was your home worth?"

"$350,000 is what it last appraised at."

"How long ago was that?"

"A year."

"How much is the insurance policy payout for a fire?"

"One million dollars."

"Why is the payout amount so much larger than the value of the house?"

"The way the insurance company explained it to me was that they had factored in all of my valuables."

"Do you have any outstanding debts?"

"No."

"And your bank account shows a balance just over $750,000, is that still accurate?"

"Yes, for now. I have to repay my bond to a friend of mine."

"Do you have any other bank accounts?"

"NO."

Mr. Hartford continued to write in his pad for about five more minutes. He finally looked up, "This sounds really good Shauntel. Is it possible that you may have left your door unlocked or a window open?"

"I don't think so, but I'm not sure."

"Is there anything else you think I should know to help us with this case?"

"Well, I have had quite a few stalking incidents over the last month. My home was broken into and trashed, my car was vandalized and threatening notes and tortured dolls have been delivered to me."

"That's very important information. Have you reported any of the incidents to the police?"

"No."

"Do you have any witnesses to any of the incidents?"

"Yes, Nate, my fiancé has witnessed some of them and my best friend Tasha."

"What I would like for you to do is to get a journal and jot down every incident you can remember over the last month. Talk to the two witnesses and see if they are willing to talk to me. I will call you in a couple of days to schedule our next meeting. Hopefully your fiancé and friend will be able to come to that meeting. It sounds like you're not very fond of attorneys and judges and that doesn't matter to me as long as you know not to let those feelings show while we're in court. Is there anything else you can think of that may be relevant to your case."

"I'm not sure if this is relevant, but I'm pregnant."

"I told you everything is relevant and the judge on this case is sympathetic to pregnant women so that works in our favor. She sponsors a program that helps youth whose parents are incarcerated.

Okay, I believe were done. If you think of anything else do not hesitate to call me at any hour. If I don't answer leave a voicemail message." He slid Shauntel his business card.

"One last thing, we have a stylist who will come and style you for court the week before the hearing, she will be giving you a call."

"I have my own stylist Mr. Hartford."

"I'm sure you do, but this stylist only styles people for business meetings and court, we'll go with her."

Shauntel walked Mr. Hartford to the door and as she let him out, he turned around to her and extended his hand for her to shake. Before she could shake it, Mr. Hartford was being slammed into the wall. Nate was pounding Mr. Hartford with blow after blow and yelling out obscenities about how he was going to kill him. Mr. Hartford was shielding his body as best as he could with his body curled up into a ball.

"He's my attorney, he's my attorney!!!" Shauntel was screaming. "Stop Nate, he's my attorney."

Nate stopped with fist in mid-air. "He's your what?" He asked out of breath.

"My attorney, Nate."

Nate jumped up off of Mr. Hartford and brushed his shirt off. Mr. Hartford was still dazed. He sat up and leaned against the wall trying to regain his composure. Shauntel walked over to Mr. Hartford, "Are you okay?"

"I think so."

"Nate, help me get him up."

Nate snatched him up and helped into the suite while Shauntel held the door.

"I'm sorry man, that situation looked real suspicious. Are you okay?"

"I'm fine, if it's one thing I learned in school, it was how to take a punch."

Mr. Hartford extended his hand and said winded, "Jackson Hartford, I take it you're Mr. Whittington."

Nate gave Shauntel a puzzled look then shook Mr. Hartford's hand, "Yes I am."

Shauntel jumped in, "Nate Mr. Hartford and I were just going over my case and he was getting more information so that he can help me beat this case. Mr. Hartford, would you like some water?"

"No, but may I use your restroom?"

"Sure." She showed him to the main bathroom.

"Nate what are you doing here?"

"I told you we had a situation so I couldn't stay at home last night so I stayed the night here." Nate looked around the suite, "The better question is what you are doing *here*?"

"I just needed to go somewhere to try to collect my thoughts. So I came here to do that."

"That's not what I meant. I meant how did you get *this* suite?"

"You know I have connections. A friend of mine called in some favors."

Mr. Hartford cleared his throat before interrupting. "Well Shauntel I'm going to get going so that I can get to work on your case."

She was grateful for the interruption. She didn't want to explain how Mike had bonded her out of jail, taken her shopping and put her up in the most fabulous suite in the whole state. She was always honest with Nate, but she never wanted to make him feel like less than a man. There were better ways to get a man to do just what you wanted him to.

Nate walked toward Mr. Hartford. "My bad man. That just didn't look right to me."

"No hard feelings Mr. Whittington, I would have probably reacted the same way if I had a woman as beautiful as Ms. Barnes. By the way, I told your fiancé that I will need to talk to you soon to get a statement and may need you as a witness for her. I will let you two discuss it and determine when a good time will be. "

****

Nate and Shauntel were lying in his bed talking about the events over the past few days. They had both checked out of their hotel rooms once Nate had the all clear from The Eye. He was happy that things would be settling down now and hoped that he and Shauntel would have time to focus on planning their future together. He had a better understanding of why she was upset and why she wasn't talking to him and she had a better understanding of why he hadn't got to the jail as quickly as she would have liked. He agreed to step his game up and be on top of things better and she agreed that she would be more patient and talk to him about any issues she had with him.

"Nate I am convinced that Byron is the one causing all of this confusion."

"Why do you think that?"

"He just exudes stalker. When we were dating, he would show up in places where I was all of the time and try to act like it was a coincidence. One day I was on a dinner date with the guy named Troy that I told you about and I looked up and noticed that Byron was across the room at another table just staring at me. When he noticed that I saw him, he gave me this creepy look. He called me as soon as I left the restaurant and started pounding me with questions. I reminded him that I was single and he wasn't my man and he got real gutter with me."

"What do you mean gutter?"

"Real dirty Nate, telling me how I wasn't saying he wasn't my man when he was doing this and doing that. He even called me out of my name. Again, I had to let him know that I didn't need his ass!!! I was well off before I met him and would still be after he was gone. Then I told him how his loving wasn't all of that anyway and he got really heated. That conversation was the end of our friendship and all of this confusion started about a week after that."

"You know you can be cold, Tel."

"I'm not cold. I just have to be honest with people and everybody can't handle the truth."

"I can handle the truth, so is my loving all of that?"

"All of that and then some!"

"Well then, let's see how much of then some."

He pulled her into his arms and kissed her with more passion than he ever had. She loved how commanding Nate was in bed. His strong firm grip had her wet in seconds and she was ready to do some much needed stress releasing. They made love for the next 5 hours non-stop. Nate was sleep within minutes of their last session. She knew he had to be up for work in a couple of hours and she couldn't sleep even after all of that activity. So, she got up to go cook a meal so that he would have some lunch for later on that night.

Shauntel was a great cook; a skill she inherited from her mother. Before her mom totally lost it, she made her money from cooking for people in the community, family and friends. Let her tell it, she didn't own a catering business. But she made good money because her food was in high demand. Shauntel cooked some NY Strip Steak, shrimp scampi, Scallop potatoes, an Italian salad and some honey butter biscuits. She fixed her plate and bit down into the steak. It was so tender that it melted in her mouth. She was only able to eat a few bites before she was full. She wrapped her plate up and put it up for later. Nate walked up behind her while she was washing dishes. He wrapped his arms around her waist planting sensual kisses on her neck. "Hey sexy, you are just too good to me."

She turned around to face him, "We're too good to each other."

They both chuckled and shared a kiss. "Tel, it smells so good in here. Girl you need to own a restaurant."

"I would love to Nate. It's just such a hassle with all of the Health Department's rules and inspections. Then you need dependable people to help run everything. I'm getting a headache just thinking about it."

"Now you know I would be right by your side helping you carry that load. As good as your food is you would be famous with locations all over the world.

You can do it babe, I believe in you. I can be your cheerleader. Give me an S," He crouched down.

She swatted at him while laughing. "Stop it."

"I'm serious, you should really think about it."

She patted his firm chest. "I will."

Nate ate a small meal, took a shower and got dressed for work. He kissed Shauntel goodbye and made her promise him that she would get some rest while he was at work.

No matter how hard she tried, Shauntel just could not get to sleep. She was getting angry as the memory of all of the horrible things she had been a victim of over the last month flashed through her mind. She picked up her cell phone with much attitude to give Byron a piece of her mind. She was even angrier when his phone went straight to voicemail. She contemplated whether or not she should leave a message until she heard the message tone indicating it was time to leave a message or hang up.

"Look Byron, I understand that you may be upset because I broke it off with you. But, you left me no choice. I was upfront and honest with you that I wasn't trying to settle down with anybody. I was just doing me. You wanted to try to lock me down and it

just wasn't going to happen. Now you are taking things too far! Vandalizing cars and setting fires is not cute. Even if I was thinking about giving you another chance, you have completely ruined it with all of this stalking. Honestly, you're acting like a little bitch! I'm only going to tell you this once, back up unless you want to be a part of a real life war. I don't play, but even more my **man** *really doesn't play. I suggest you chuck it up as a lost and keep it moving unless you want to meet your maker. And another thing.......*"

The message tone beeped again indicating that there was no time left to finish the message. She growled with frustration as she hung up the phone. Five minutes later her phone was ringing. She looked at the caller ID and saw it was Byron.

She pushed the talk button. "What?" She huffed through the phone.

"First of all Shauntel, you need to calm down because you're on some other shit!"

She was screaming now. "I'm not *on* anything Byron. You're the one who must be *on* something. I am sick and tired of all of this! You got a problem with me then be a man about it and see me on it. All of this stalking and burning down houses and shit is some bitch shit."

He interrupted calmly, "I have no idea what you're talking about. I'm not stalking anybody. You said something on my voicemail about vandalizing cars. I'm not even cut like that and you should know that. Shauntel I love you and I still want you to be mine. I would never do anything scandalous like that to you. Why do I have to be a bitch though?"

She heard crying is his voice, "I know you're not crying."

He was sniffling, "Shauntel I fell in love with you hard. I was trying to 'keep it friendly' like you would always say. But it's something about you and I'm not sure what it is. I moved to Atlanta to get my mind off of you a couple of weeks after our last conversation. I still can't stop thinking about you and I was hoping that you would move down here with me."

She burst into laughter, "Move down there with you? Look Byron I am engaged to be married. I told you that there would never be an *us* and there never will be."

There was anger in his voice now, "Oh so you can marry some other dude but you can't be mine? I don't know who is stalking you but I hope they don't stop because you're a dirty bitch." he hung up in her face.

She was even more convinced now that she knew for sure that Byron was crazy and was probably the stalker. He had to be lying about moving to Atlanta. The way he went from mad to sad and loving then to downright disrespectful, had her thinking he had a mental problem for real. She felt nauseous all of a sudden and took off running to the bathroom. She just barely made it to toilet before she threw up. This was the first actual sign of her pregnancy. She cleaned herself up and then had an urgency to pee. She noticed that she was bleeding after she was done. She called Nate but he didn't answer the phone so she left him a voicemail letting him know that she was going to the emergency room. Then she called Tasha and asked her to come take her to the hospital because she didn't want to drive not knowing what was going on with the baby.

CHAPTER 5

Tasha wasn't the prettiest girl, but she was not ugly. Most would classify her as average looking. She had a small frame including a small waist and heavy top. She began to develop up top in the 5th grade and that's when all of the boys started to notice her. From the 5th grade and on, her rack always impressed the opposite sex. She was light skinned with really full lips too so most men always looked at her as a sex toy. She had always been a little envious of Shauntel because she felt like Shauntel always came up with the longer end of the stick. Even though they both had grown up without their parents', at least Shauntel had her grandmother there for her.

Tasha's whole family was filled with a bunch of losers in her opinion. None of them ever checked on her to see if she was alright after her mother died. Had it not been for Shauntel's grandmother, she would have been on her own. It was very painful for none of her family to even show up for her High School graduation. It was on prom night that her jealousy for Shauntel had turn into pure envy. She had been harboring ill feelings for more than ten years until recently. One Sunday morning recently though, she woke up and decided that she was going to church. During the service, it seemed like the preacher's whole message was directed at her. He spoke of how jealousy and bitterness only hurts the person who had those feelings toward another. He preached about forgiveness and how the Lord expects us to forgive in order to be forgiven. By the end of the sermon, Tasha was in tears. It was like a light came on and showed her herself. She had been so angry, jealous and bitter towards so many people. She made her way to the altar and left all of those negative emotions right there. It was like a thousand pound weight had been lifted from her heart. After that, she had a new love for Shauntel and really wanted to tell her all about it, but so much drama had been going on that they really hadn't had time to sit and have a real conversation. Plus she wasn't sure how Shauntel would take it.

Tasha grabbed her keys and made her way to her car to go take her best sister friend to the emergency room. For once the hospital was pretty clear so they did not have to wait to go to the back and get a room. Within 10 minutes of their arrival, the nurse had already drawn Shauntel's blood and let her know that the Doctor would be in to examine her soon. Nate was at the hospital 20 minutes after they were. He hated hospitals but he refused to fall short again especially on something this important. He had left Corey in charge of security at the club after he heard Shauntel's voicemail. He was right at her side rubbing her back when Tasha came back to the room from getting some coffee. She just stood there and smiled. She was so happy for the love that she had envied until recently. The Doctor came in and asked Tasha and Nate to step out so that he could do a vaginal examination and they did.

While they waited in the lobby Tasha decided she would try to talk to Nate about the situation since he knew Shauntel better than anyone. "Nate I need to talk to somebody about some things that I have going on and since you are almost my brother-in-law, maybe you could give me some advice."

"Sure, what's up T?"

"Well, you know that I love Shauntel like we have the same momma and daddy."

"Yeah."

"Well up until recently I had been really jealous of Shauntel. I mean I never loved her any less. I just felt like she was always more fortunate than me. It always seemed that she took things for granted. Another thing that really had me upset was her confidence. I have done some really bad things to her and I need her to forgive me."

"How can you love somebody and be jealous of them?"

"I'm trying to explain that to you now, if you'd listen."

"My bad."

"Recently I went to a church service and had what they call a revelation. I was so angry and upset from all of the crazy things that went on in my childhood that I had turned into an emotional wreck. I realized that I was not only taking this out on Shauntel but on everybody in my life including myself. I have sabotaged every romantic relationship I have ever had. Well I had a life changing experience that day and I really am a new person. God delivered me from all of those negative feelings. Now I feel like I need to share this with Shauntel. She is the closest person to me on earth."

"You know how Shauntel is. I'm sure she will be able to understand. Just do me a favor and wait until we come back from vacation to drop this on her. I'm going to take her out of town in a couple of days so that she can actually get some rest."

"Thanks for listening Nate. I am really am happy for you two and I know that you are exactly the man she needs."

"Thanks Tasha and thanks for bringing her to the hospital."

The Doctor came out and motioned for them to follow him back into Shauntel's room. Once they were all settled in, he told them, "Ms. Barnes wanted you two back in here before I told her anything. I have some news. Ms. Barnes, your cervix is not dilated which is great news." Nate grabbed her hand, dropped his head and exhaled loudly. The Doctor Continued, "Now we just need to get the results of your HCG blood test and do one more test. I am going to have an ultrasound done just to make sure that things are looking ok in there. If you need anything, let the nurse know and I will see you in about an hour." He tapped Shauntel's blanket for encouragement and left.

About 15 minutes later a transporter came into the room and asked Shauntel if she was ready to go for her ultrasound. "As ready as I'm going to be." He gathered the bag with her belongings in it and tucked it securely under her bed. Then he wheeled her to the Radiology section of the hospital. "Wait right here. I just have to let the technician know that you're here and give her your chart." The attendant disappeared into the room for about two minutes. He came back out with a Barbie looking ultrasound technician. She even spoke like a Barbie doll. "Hello Ms. Barnes, I'm Rebecca, the ultrasound tech. Have you ever had an ultrasound?" She asked smiling.

"Hi. No I haven't."

"You ready?"

"Yes, but can my fiancé come in with me.?"

"Sure he can."

The technician wheeled Shauntel into the room with Nate in tow. She locked the bed in place and began to explain the procedure to Shauntel. "This procedure is pretty simple. There is little to no discomfort. I can explain different features of the baby as they show on this screen. However, I am not able to tell you any medical results. I'm just the photographer." She laughed.

Shauntel was happy for the humor. It helped to ease her stress a bit. The Technician put a plastic cover over the funny shaped ultrasound tool, squeezed a gel substance onto it and began to insert it into Shauntel. "Just relax. The more you relax the less discomfort there will be."

Shauntel took a deep breath and the tech gently inserted the whole tool inside her.

"Now that wasn't so bad was it?"

"I guess not."

The tech turned on the ultrasound machine and picture of the baby popped on the screen. Shauntel's heart melted. Nate was amazed and it showed on his face. He started pounding the tech with questions, "Is that his?" and "What is that?" All the while the tech kept her professional demeanor and Barbie like smile answering all of the questions that weren't medical related. After she had all the pictures she needed. She let them hear the baby's heartbeat. They were both blown away.

The tech told Shauntel that she would be getting the pictures over to the Doctor right away so she should be hearing something really soon. The transporter came back a few minutes later and wheeled her back to her room. He made sure she was comfortable and that nobody needed anything. They turned on the TV and were all watching when Nate tapped Shauntel. "Tel I really think that there is just too much stress for you here right now. As soon as they let you go. I want to take you on a short vacation so that you can really relax. The baby and me need you to get better. The baby, so that he can get better and me, so that I can get you wetter."

"Boy you are so nasty. That sounds like a really good idea though Nate. I really could use a vacation. We don't know how long I'm going to have to be here though."

"I know but however long it takes, I'm taking you away from all of this confusion as soon as you are released."

The Doctor walked in twenty minutes later with Shauntel's chart in his hand. "How are you feeling Ms. Barnes?"

"Besides cold and hungry, I'm fine."

"I can have the nurse to bring you a snack."

"No thanks even though I'm hungry, I'm too nervous to eat right now," she told him while playing with her hair.

"Okay. All of your test results are back and everything looks good. Your HCG levels are normal and your ultrasound shows that the baby looks healthy."

Shauntel breathed a breath of relief, "What caused the bleeding Doctor?"

"We can't be absolutely sure. The good thing is that the life threatening things are not present. My guess would be stress. Do you have a lot going on?"

"You wouldn't believe me if I told you."

"Well I am ordering you to bed rest for four weeks. That means that you are to do nothing strenuous including sex. It will be better explained in your discharge papers. I will release you if you promise to follow my orders."

"Of course I will Doctor I will do anything to get out of here."

He smiled, "I'm sure you would Ms. Barnes. Do you want to know the sex of the baby?"

Nate said yes and Shauntel said no at the same time. There was a brief silence. Shauntel broke it,

"You can tell him in private as long as he promises not to tell me." "Okay, I'm going to go prepare your discharge papers. I will have the nurse bring you a warm blanket. Do you all need anything else?"

Nate jumped in, "I have a question Doctor Is she able to travel at all?"

It depends on the type of travel. As long as she is able to rest during the travel and it is a short distance she should be ok. No airplane, train or bus rides."

"Will that be included in the discharge papers?"

"I can have them add travel instructions."

"Thanks Doctor."

"You're welcome. You will need to follow up with your OB/GYN at the end of the four weeks. If you have any more complications between then and now please come back to the emergency room. Feel better Ms. Barnes." Nate and the Doctor walked out of the room.

****

On the way to Nate's house, Shauntel told Nate about the conversation that she had with Byron. Nate was furious that Byron had been so disrespectful to

Shauntel and he planned to handle that as soon as their vacation was over. It was the middle of the night so it was dark when Nate and Shauntel pulled up to his house. So, they didn't notice the damage to the house until they were out of the car and on their way to the door. Every last window in the condo was broken out and the front had 'How does it feel to be inside my woman?' spray-painted in red on it. Nate had a sinking feeling in his stomach that maybe The Eye hadn't been so thorough in making sure that the problem had been solved. He told Shauntel to get back in the car and lock the doors. She did.

Nate went inside to see how much damage had been done. Thankfully, the only damage was on the outside. He grabbed his luggage and filled it with enough things for him and Shauntel to make it through the night. He knew that it would be too cold to stay there with all of the windows gone. As he was loading the luggage into the trunk, he heard a loud noise behind his house. He pulled out his Glock and walked toward the back of the house when a gunshot came flying his way. He ducked down and put his body up against the side of the house. He saw a dark silhouette running away from the house. He let off two shots just as the silhouette disappeared over the fence that led to the alley. He jumped in the car and made sure Shauntel was alright before he drove to the Iced Hotel of Detroit and rented them a suite. He figured the sooner Shauntel could lay down, the better.

All Shauntel wanted to do was sleep. She was just so shook from bullets flying at her that she didn't think that she would be able to. Nate ran her a hot bath and got to work on his master plan. The first thing he did was call The Eye and left a message, "*Yo, I need to talk". Give me a call as soon as you get this message.*" The Eye had so many different code terms. Nate actually thought that it was ridiculous for a grown man to be running around using code words, but he had to follow the rules and The Eye was the best. He knew that "*I need to talk*" meant that it was an emergency situation.

Then he pulled out his laptop and searched vacation destinations that were within driving distance. He found four to choose from and left all four windows open for Shauntel to make a decision when she got out of the tub. He then gathered the telephone numbers for all of the people he needed to call in the morning. He knew that he would not get any sleep that night, there was just too much on his mind.

Shauntel came out wearing the plush hotel robe and a towel on her head glowing with perfection. He massaged her body down with her favorite vanilla oil, encouraging her to relax the whole time. By the time he was finished she was lightly snoring. He lay there in awe that she was even more beautiful when she was sleep when his phone ringing jarred him from his thoughts. He quickly pressed the answer key and left the room so he wouldn't disturb Shauntel.

"Hello?"

"You need to talk?"

"Yeah, like yesterday."

"Meet me at the office at 3:00 sharp."

"Bet."

Nate hung up the phone and looked at the clock it was 5 am. The Eye's code rule was to subtract the time he said to meet from 12:00. That translated to 12 minus 3. 3:00 sharp meant 9:00 sharp so he had 4 hours. Nate hopped in the shower, got out and ironed his clothes to kill time. He watched the news until about 7:30. Then he decided to order up some breakfast so that Shauntel would have something to eat when she woke up. At 8:00 he left her breakfast and the laptop on the hotel nightstand with a note:

"I have to go and take care of some business. I left the laptop here with four different vacation places that are within driving distance. You pick. If you need anything, call me. Enjoy your breakfast. See you soon."

Nate was at "The Office" by 8:20. The Office was actually a little deserted park down in Southwest Detroit. He sat and waited because he knew that The Eye was always early and they needed to have this conversation ASAP.

Since he would have to wait for a while, Nate started making phone calls. First he called his friend Pete who owned his own spy shop. He told him that he needed a surveillance system setup at his house immediately. Pete told him to meet him there at 2:00. Nate's first instinct was to call the insurance company next, but he figured it would be cheaper in the long run to just replace the windows and door himself. Claims always made your insurance premium higher. So he hopped on his phone's internet browser and found the number to the best window company in town. He called and made an appointment for 3:00 to have his windows and door replaced. He knew that Corey would still be sleep so he dialed straight into his voicemail and left him a message telling him to give him a call when he got up. Then he called Tasha and told her that he needed her to go and keep Shauntel company and to help her out if she needed anything while he was out.

As usual, The Eye observed his surroundings to make sure that everything was kosher. Then he walked up to Nate's passenger door and got into the car.

"What's up Nate?"

"We've got a problem."

"There's a solution to every problem, my man. What's the issue?"

"My house was vandalized last night which suggests that maybe our little problem is back."

"Well I've got my guy on him every few days to make sure that he stays away. The last I heard, the problem was still in Ohio."

The Eye had called up one of his fellow Army buddies who lived in Ohio to make sure that the guy was still living there and not on his way back to Detroit to cause any trouble.

"How long ago was that?"

"That was the day before yesterday. I'll call him and check now."

The Eye pushed a speed dial key on his phone and then put the call on speakerphone.

"Hello?"

"How are things going?"

"The sun is shining and there's a nice breeze."
"Are the ducks sitting?"

"Sitting pretty."

"When was the last time you've been to the pond?"

"A few hours ago."

"Cool, later," The Eye disconnected the call.

He looked at Nate, "told you."

Nate looked perplexed. He was in deep thought. He was realizing that Byron had to be the culprit. He didn't want to get his hands dirty and risk his own freedom when he knew The Eye could handle it and not leave a single trail. So he made a deal to put a permanent end to all of this. He gave The Eye all of Byron's information and they agreed that Byron would be erased by the time Nate and Shauntel got back from vacation.

CHAPTER 6

*T*he Eye wasn't the kind of guy you met every day. He had skills and intelligence that most men only dreamed about. Born Elijah Taylor, the youngest child of a military family, he felt the pressure to succeed in everything he took on. When he graduated from High School, he had many scholarships. However, he felt obligated to go to the military since everyone else in his family had. So he enlisted in the army at the ripe age of 18 and it wasn't long before he was enrolled in Special Forces training. Most things had come easy to him, but the military wasn't so easy and it made him feel like he was home. He did go to college while in the Army. He majored in military investigations and graduated with honors.

The Eye's army unit noticed how keen he was when they were pinned down in a village in Kuwait during the gulf war. They had radioed for back up and the backup was near according to radio transmissions. As backup approached and his group got excited, Elijah noticed something wasn't right. The backup soldiers were wearing the same fatigues as they were, but they were all wearing ghutras on their heads. Americans do not wear ghutras. Elijah's intuition kicked in and he warned his unit that they were being setup. Because of Elijah's observation and quick response, all of the soldiers' lives were saved. They had one soldier take a bullet but the injury was not life threatening. That event got him the appreciative nickname, The Eye.

Elijah continued working Special Forces half of his time and worked as a Military Police Investigator the other half. By the time he was 21, he had too many medals and commendations to name. He went on to eventually become a colonel. After serving 15 years he was honorably discharged and started his own Private Investigation firm. He was doing great until his parents were killed in a robbery gone wrong at their family jewelry store business a year later. Things seemed to take an angry turn in his life.

Deep down Elijah wanted revenge on the man who took his parents' lives. Unfortunately he would never get that chance because the guy was sentenced to life without the possibility of parole. Not long after that, Elijah got into the murder for hire business. That was how he dealt with his vengeful feelings. He imagined that every person he took out was the guy who killed his parents. He used his PI business as a cover. He was so good at what he did that he was able to charge hefty fees to erase people. His clients knew that he was the best. He was a former Green Beret and could kill a man with his bare hands after all. They also felt secure in never being found out because thorough was an understatement for The Eye.

The Eye watched Byron get into his Cadillac Escalade and pull off. He waited five minutes before he pulled off in the direction that the GPS tracker receiver showed Byron was traveling. He had placed the tracker under the escalade near the exhaust system, just like he always did when he needed to track someone's location. He was driving for 20 minutes before the receiver showed that Byron had stopped at a soul food restaurant downtown. Five minutes later, The Eye pulled into a parking spot about half a block behind Byron. The Eye waited patiently for Byron to resurface 30 minutes later. He waited another five minutes for the receiver to give him direction before continuing to follow him. They ended up on a residential street on the Westside. The Eye pulled over on the corner of the side street so that he could see what Byron was doing without being spotted. He committed the address to memory while he waited to see if this was going to be Byron's resting place for the evening. Five minutes later Byron and a pretty young lady walked back to his SUV and Byron pulled off. He continued to follow them, making sure to keep at least a five-minute distance between them. They arrived at their destination about 15 minutes later. It was a spectacular home in Rosedale Park. The Eye staked the place out for an hour then decided that this must be Byron's home. He went home and set the receiver to send a notification in case of any movement. He figured he'd get some rest because he would need to trail Byron for the next few days in order to effectively do the job.

****

Junior was a neighborhood thug who really had no street credit or heart. He would rob people who were helpless and take the money to go get high. His imagination was astronomical so he would always tell lies to make himself look good. Most people always knew when he was lying though because he was horrible at it. On top of telling unbelievable stories about his so called fabulous life, he would always stutter and rub his nose when he lied. He had a new scheme every week. His life hadn't always been so pathetic. He was a nerd with a lot of potential in High School. He got caught up with the wrong crowd in his senior year and lost all of his possibilities of going to college on a full scholarship.

Junior grew up with Tasha and Shauntel. He had always had a huge crush on Tasha, but she never liked him. Recently though, she had used his fondness of her to recruit him for her own agenda. Tasha hated even having to be in his presence, but she had to straighten out the mess she had created. She had just seen Nate and Shauntel off for their vacation and she was feeling even guiltier about her actions now.

She was meeting Junior at an abandoned warehouse on the south side of town where they had met in the past. Junior walked in looking like he had been wearing his clothes for at least three days. His clothes were wrinkled and he had an odor about him.

"What's up Ma?"

"Junior we need to talk!"

"No hello? No how you doing?"

"Look, I don't have time for small talk."

He stuttered and rubbed his nose. "Well I'm doing... doing real good... good out here get... getting this bread even though you didn't ask."

"Anyway Junior, what the hell is going on?"

"What do you mean?"

"Why are you stalking Shauntel and doing all this crazy shit?"

"I don't know what you're talking about Tasha. I am not stalking Shauntel. I did what you asked me to and that was the end of it for me Ma."

"Listen I'm not playing with you Junior. You have to stop it now before somebody gets hurt."

"Like I said I only did that one job and I'm still waiting for my payment on that. So when are we going on this *one* date?"

Just then it dawned on Tasha that Junior wasn't stuttering or rubbing his nose like he always did when he was lying. He must be telling the truth. Tasha was disturbed now, because she had no idea who would really want to put Shauntel through all of that. Junior moved closer to her and his smell broke her from her thoughts.

"Junior I have a lot going on so I cannot think about that *one* date right now."

He stepped even closer, "Maybe we can go on that date right now then, I don't see much going on in here."

She took a step backward to escape his not so pleasant smell, "First of all Junior you would need to take 100 showers, get off of dope and get tested for a million diseases before I even think about going out with you."

He grabbed her arm, "So you were just playing me?"

She snatched away from him, "Let me go, you should've known better. Did you really think I would go out with a dope fiend?"

He slapped her across the face so hard that it felt like her whole head spun around. Once she was able to see again, she started swinging like a madwoman. Junior was fast though and he was able to avoid the majority of her swings until he finally just gave her an uppercut to the stomach. She toppled over. He shoved her to the ground hard and her head hit the cement knocking her out.

By this time Junior was seething as he jumped on top of her and started ripping her clothes off. He was murmuring "You knew I been wanting this all these years Bitch! But you like to tease me. You gonna give me some of this ass today!" He smothered her mouth with his, despite her unconsciousness. As he was engulfed in his solo kiss, he was pulling out his 8-1/2 inch dick.

Tasha was still out of it until he slammed all 8-1/2 inches inside of her at once. The piercing pain in her vagina snatched her awake and she instantly began to swing and scream. "Get the fuck off of me!" Junior pinned both of her hands over her head with one hand and covered her mouth with his other one. He continued to pound her fiercely and verbally abuse her for the next 10 minutes. It felt more like 10 days to her. Once he was done, he snatched his member out of her, fixed his clothes and walked out like he was just doing a normal daily activity.

Tasha lay there in shock with tears streaming down her face. She was numb and it felt like she couldn't move if she wanted to. After a few minutes, she forced herself to get up off of the hard cement and stumbled to her car. She fell into the driver's seat and sat crying for the next two hours contemplating what her next move needed to be.

****

Nate had a busy day the day before. He had his motion detector surveillance system installed on the house and all 21 of his windows replaced. The door had been replaced but he sent the old door out for painting and planned to keep it as a spare in the garage. He made the reservations at the Resort Spa in Illinois that Shauntel had decided on. He had met with Corey and made sure he had everything he needed to handle all of the security business and Corey agreed to keep a watch over Nate's house. Then he went shopping and bought everything they would need for the trip including all of the clothes Shauntel would need to make it through their seven day stay. He was exhausted and decided that they would leave the next morning since he hadn't had any sleep. Now they were on the road and on their way to finally relax.

He had reserved the rooftop suite, which included a beautiful view, fully stocked kitchen, enchanting balcony and fireplace just to name a few amenities. Shauntel slept most of the way aside from the one time they stopped to go to the bathroom and get something to eat. He had rented an extended SUV and made a makeshift bed in the back seat so that she could lie down comfortably. They arrived at the hotel just after 2 o'clock in the afternoon after the 5-hour drive.

Nate went in to register and get the room key. The lobby was gorgeous with 100-foot ceilings and walls trimmed in cherry wood.

The floor was covered with ceramic tiles that complimented the color scheme of reds, golds, oranges and browns. There was fascinating antique art on the walls and balconies where guests could overlook the lobby from their floors. There were many seating areas including a long dining table that sat ten and the most charming white brick fireplace. The air smelt clean and fresh with a spa feel to it. He approached the desk and greeted the soft-spoken guest services clerk. She gave him his room keys and approved his early check in. He was amazed at the relaxing aura of the hotel. He couldn't wait to get Shauntel inside for some relaxation.

Once they were settled in, they took turns taking showers. He ordered room service while Shauntel was in the shower. They had a beautiful fruit basket that included grapes, strawberries, watermelon, cherries, kiwi and pineapples. There was a tray of chocolate covered cherries, roasted almonds, English toffee, pistachios and European chocolate. There was another tray with herbal teas and hot water. The main course was shrimp scampi, French three onion soup and cheese biscuits. He also ordered a few bottles of non-alcoholic champagne. They sat and snacked on the fruit and other snacks while watching a movie. When the movie went off, they sat at the dining table and ate dinner while having a long conversation about their future. When they were done they had set a date for their wedding. They had a few prospective venues and Shauntel had decided to really consider going into the restaurant business.

Nate cleaned the kitchen while Shauntel looked for another good movie for them to watch. They cuddled while they watched another movie together and then went to bed. The relaxation had started and would continue for the next six days. He had an all-inclusive spa visited planned for the next day.

****

The Eye had been tailing Byron for the last three days in order to become familiar with his routine. Unlike most people though, Byron's life was anything but routine. He was all over the place all three days. He didn't seem to have a job or any income building activity at all. The Eye was starting to wonder how he was able to live within the means that he was living in. He decided that he would have to improvise on this job since there was no predictability. So he had parked his car a couple blocks over from Byron's house in a recreational center's parking lot being careful to remain out of the sight of the center's cameras. He then cut through the houses to the back of Byron's house and picked the back door's lock and let himself in. Once inside, he had a better understanding about Byron's financial situation. The only furniture in the big luxury house was a living room chair, a small colored television and an old rickety dining room table. The Eye sat in the dark in the living room chair with his gun in his lap awaiting Byron's arrival. He had been sure to keep on his rubber gloves, attach the silencer to his gun and remove his boots before entering the house. He had been waiting since eight o'clock and his watch now read 11:37. He was starting to worry that Byron might not come home when he heard the truck pulling into the driveway. A couple minutes later Byron opened the door and as soon as he walked from the foyer into the living room, The Eye had his Walther PPK trained on him. In a split second Byron was shot in the heart. The Eye walked over to Byron, stood over him and shot him again in the head. He walked to the back of the house and peeped out to make sure there was no movement. He stepped outside and put his shoes back on. Then he took the same route back to his car and was gone like a thief in the night.

****

Tasha was still dazed and confused as she sat outside of her house. She had no idea what she should do. The only family she had was

Shauntel and she didn't want to ruin her relaxing vacation. She knew that if she called the police they were going to want to poke and pry. She really was too exhausted to go through all of that. If she went to the

106

hospital or a rape counseling center she would have to deal with the similar pestering. She wanted revenge on Junior for what he had done to her but she didn't want to go through all of the horrible court sessions to get that justice. She wanted to cry but she had been crying for so long that no more tears would come out. She started banging her head on her steering wheel hoping the pain in her head would counter the pain in her heart. Just then a radio advertisement came on "Are you in a sexually abusive relationship? Have you been a victim of molestation or date rape? Do you feel that there's no one there to help you? You are not alone. We are here to assist you. At the Community Counseling Center Your secrets are safe with us. We have professionally trained Counselors here to listen and give advice. Here you are safe and secure. We are open 24 hours give us a call at......." Tasha took this as a sign. She started scrambling through her glove box to find an ink pen to write down the telephone number. She couldn't find one, so she snatched her cell phone from her purse and punched the number in just as the lady announcer was finishing up the phone number for the second time. "Call now."

Tasha contemplated on pushing the dial button. The advertisement had to be a sign from God, so she pushed the dial button. The voice on the other end was calm and soothing "Community Counseling Center, this is April may I have your name please?"

Tasha was a little apprehensive, "Uh, my name is Tasha."

"Hi Tasha, I am April and I'm here to help in any way you need me to. Is there anything in particular you want to talk about today?"

Tasha took a deep breath and almost screamed out "I was raped!"

The counselor waited a few seconds, "Tasha, are you in a safe place?"

"Yes."

"Did you know your attacker?"

"Yes, he..." Tasha lost her wording and despite her earlier assessment of no more tears, she began to sob uncontrollably.

The counselor was calm and quiet for a few more seconds. Then she said, "It's okay Tasha let it all out. Crying is good."

Tasha was thinking to herself, *this lady must be crazy, how in the world is crying good*?

She tried between sobs to tell the counselor, "I'm sorry."

The counselor spoke again, "Tasha I am here for you and have all the patience in the world. It is never good to bottle our feelings up inside. Crying is a cleansing method."

After a few minutes, Tasha was able to get her thoughts out, "He was a guy I went to school with. He beat me and raped me. I have never had anything like this happen to me." Then she screamed, "How could he do this to me? I know I used him and told him that I would go on a date with him. But did I deserve this?"

"No Tasha. You did not deserve that. No matter what you did, it is never okay for anyone to hurt you physically."

"I don't know what to do. I can't tell anybody this!" Then she said like she was delivering news to herself, "Oh my God, I was raped!"

"Tasha, would you be willing to come into my office?"

"I'm not sure that I can make it anywhere."

"Where are you now?"

"I'm in my car in my driveway."

"I can come to you if you prefer."

"No. I should be able to make it to you if you give me a few minutes to get myself together."

"Take all the time you need."

About five minutes later Tasha told her, "I can make it."

"Okay, I can stay on the phone with you and lead you here. Tell me where you're coming from."

The counselor stayed on the phone with Tasha until she made it to the counseling center. She told Tasha to let the receptionist know that she would be expecting her. Tasha walked up to the quaint isolated building and rang the bell. The receptionist came over the intercom. "How may I help you?"

"My name is Tasha and April is expecting me."

The door buzzed and Tasha let herself in. She walked into the building and noticed how outdated it looked. The floors squeaked under her feet as she walked up the three steps into the office. She was beginning to have second thoughts when the receptionist said, "Follow me Tasha." She did as she was told and followed the receptionist down the narrow poorly lit hallway to an office at the end of the building. The counselor was a caramel colored very tall skinny woman. She could have passed for a model except that her fashion sense was non-existent. She had on a khaki A-line skirt that fell just below the knee, a white frilly blouse with a plum sweater draped across her back with the sleeves hanging in the front of her blouse and some brown baby doll shoes. Her glasses looked like they came from the free rack. The only thing that showed a hint of the 21st century was her long black flowing hair weave.

The counselor motioned for Tasha to sit down. "Have a seat Tasha. Would you like a bottled water?" Tasha shook her head no.

The therapist looked at her intently, "How about we start from the beginning."

Tasha went on to tell her how she had developed a strong jealousy for her best friend and how that had caused her to enlist Junior to trash Shauntel's house. She also told her about the church service that had helped her to work through her envious feelings and bring about regrets. Then she told her how she had arranged the meeting at the old warehouse with Junior and all of the details of the rape. The counselor listened attentively the whole time Tasha was speaking. The she asked, "How do you feel right now?"

Tasha shrugged her shoulders. "I'm not really sure. Mostly numb."

"That's normal. You have just been through a really traumatic experience. You will probably start experiencing a roller coaster of emotions soon. The best thing to do is to deal with those emotions as they come. Recognize them for what they are and consider exactly what is causing the emotion and work to fix the cause. All emotions have an underlying cause. For instance if you find yourself angry, ask yourself what is it exactly that you are angry about. Then deal with the answer to that question. The more you do this, the better you will become at it. The most important thing that I want you to remember is that this is not your fault. If you are not convinced of that, then tell yourself that every day as many times as necessary."

Tasha nodded in agreement. The therapist took a long pause waiting to see if Tasha had anything she wanted to add. After Tasha gave no response, the therapist continued, "Have you thought about whether or not you want to report this attack to the police?"

"I have thought about it, but I'm not sure what I want to do. I really don't want him to get away with this, but I also don't want to have to go through all of the embarrassment that will come if I report it."

"That's understandable Tasha."

"What do you think I should do?"

"That's not a question I can answer for you. However, if I were in your position I would report it. There is a way that we can remedy this temporarily though. You could go to our Doctor at the Hospital and have the rape examination so that if you decide later to pursue rape charges, the state will have all of the physical evidence they will need to proceed. I will even go with you for moral support."

Tasha thought about it for a minute then exhaled an "Okay."

CHAPTER 7

Nate and Shauntel both lay next to each other on separate massage tables faced down enjoying their full body massages. They were having a barely audible conversation because of the pleasure they were both experiencing. "Thank you for thinking of this Nate. I really needed this."

"That's what I'm here for. I always know what you need. I'm just glad that when we get back to Detroit all of this will be over."

"How do you know?"

"Trust me. I took care of it for you."

Shauntel didn't like the sound of that, but she decided against prying any further. She didn't want to ruin her relaxation massage with any negativity. Instead she focused on the positive. "Nate while you were out golfing this morning, I did some research on starting the restaurant business."

"Yeah? What did you find out?"
"It's not nearly as difficult as I thought it would be and I really think that I want to do it."

"If you're serious, I know just the right person to call to get it off of the ground successfully."

"Really?"

"Yep. You know that I'm really good at putting the right people together."

"Yes you are. I was thinking maybe we could do this as a partnership and name it something catchy that symbolizes our union."

"You mean something like Tel-Nate?"

"Yeah, but not so corny." They both laughed.

"Okay then you come up with something better."

"How about The Whittington Barn?" "That sounds upscale, just a little long. How about Foxy Barn?"

"That sounds like a strip club."

"Well at least that would draw in customers. Everybody loves a good strip club. You could have strippers dressed like farm animals after dark."

"Would you be serious?"

"Ok Tel, I'm sorry. You are the creative one, not me."

"I've got it! Nate's Barn!"

"That's good, but are you trying to turn me into the woman by making me take your last name?"

"Yes Mr. Barnes."

They shared a laugh and continued chatting throughout their massages. At one point Nate grabbed her hand and just gazed into her eyes for a few minutes. He never imagined he could love anybody as much as he loved Shauntel. He was willing to die for her and she was able to read his thoughts in their gaze.

****

Shauntel knew that it was best for her to follow her doctor's instruction for bed rest but she was tired of being in the bed and she was horny as hell! Since Nate was gone out to get them something to eat, following the no sex order was easy at the moment. She powered on her laptop and went onto the Detroit News website. She wanted to catch up on anything she may have missed. She was browsing through the latest news when she saw a video link that said "Man Executed on the West Side of Detroit". She clicked on the video and the pretty petite newswoman began her story.

"Police are still trying to piece together the details of an execution style murder in the heart of Rosedale Park. Thirty Five year old Byron Stewart was found murdered in his West Detroit Home with two bullet wounds. One to the chest and one to the head."

Shauntel gasped and put her hand over her mouth.

The news reporter continued. A picture that she had seen on Byron's mantle flashed across the screen.

"Authorities are following up on a number of leads. Police say that Mr. Stewart was killed two nights ago between midnight and 2 AM. Police discovered his body this morning after his neighbor noticed that his porch light had been left on for two days and a slightly foul odor was coming from inside his house. The neighbor decided to dial 911. Detectives are not sure if there was any forced entry yet. If you have any information about this crime, please call Crime Stoppers at......."

The truth was that the police did not have one lead on what may have happened to Byron. They didn't want to sound incompetent so of course they gave the media the normal bull of having numerous leads.

117

Shauntel slammed the laptop shut and started fidgeting through the sheets to find her cell phone. She pressed number 2 on her speed dial. A few seconds later Tasha answered the phone exasperatedly. "Hello."

"What's wrong Tasha?"

"Nothing. Why you ask me that?"

"You sound down."

"I'm all good."

"No you're not."

"It's nothing to worry about. I'll tell you about it when you get home. What's up?"

"I just saw a news report online that said that Byron was murdered execution style."

"What? When?"

"The news reporter said two days ago."

"Let me pull up the video. What's the u-r-l?" Shauntel gave it to her and she pulled up the website and watched the video.

"Oh my God! What the hell was he into to be killed execution style?"

"I'm not sure, but Byron was a little off. I noticed how much right before we left. Actually I believe that he was the one stalking me."

"Why do you think that?"

"He called me telling me that he moved to Atlanta and he wanted me to move down there with him. When I told him that was not going to happen and that I was engaged, he went berserk. Obviously he was lying about moving to Atlanta and why would he need to do that if he wasn't the one doing the stalking."

"That makes sense. Not to speak ill of the dead, but at least you won't have to deal with that any more when you get back."

"That sounds all too familiar Tasha and that's why I'm worried."

"What do you mean?"

"I can't go into it right now. We have to get together as soon as I get back so that we can get caught up."

"Okay I'll make us dinner."

"Uhhhh.... Girl you know you can't cook. I'll pass on the dinner."

"Whatever! Well you can't cook while you're on bed rest."

"I know. Why don't you come over to Nate's and we can order some takeout."

"That sounds cool."

"It's a date. And Tasha don't try to play me I know that something is wrong with you and you just don't want to tell me."

"I just don't want to ruin your relaxation vacation. This time is supposed to be stress free for you. You will have more than enough to deal with when you get back. We'll talk about it then. When will you be back?"

"In two days."

"I'll see you then."

"Okay." They ended the call.

Tasha had made up her mind to tell Shauntel everything when she got home. But now that it was official that Byron had been the one doing the stalking, she figured that she'd let sleeping dogs lie. She didn't see any use in putting any strain on her and Shauntel's relationship unnecessarily.

****

Nate walked into the hotel room looking as tasty as ever. His bright white wife beater contrasted perfectly against his sexy dark skin and showed off his large muscular arms and six-pack. His outfit was perfectly coordinated with black, grey and white plaid shorts and black polo canvas shoes. Shauntel was instantly heated just from looking at him. She gazed up at him. "Good thing I trust you or I wouldn't be able to let you go outside looking and smelling that good." She breathed in the scent of his cologne.

"Baby you know that I only belong to you." He leaned down and kissed her on her forehead. "You ready to eat?"

"I was until you just came in here and started this three alarm fire."

She grabbed his hand and placed it between her legs. The heat that was penetrating from her body instantly made him stand at attention. "Tel, you know that the doctor ordered you not to have sex. Don't make it even harder for me."

She pulled his face down to hers with both hands and gave him a gentle kiss on the lips. Then she whispered in his ear. "He didn't say we couldn't use our mouths."

Nate thought about it for half of a second. "He sure didn't."

He took his shirt off. She unbuttoned his shorts and unzipped them with her teeth. They dropped to the floor. He looked so sexy in nothing but his boxer briefs. She wished she had enough patience to take a picture of him. But Shauntel was on fire with desire for him so she got on her knees in front of him and pulled his member out through the whole in the boxer briefs and went to work with pleasing him. She loved to please him. It made her even hotter when she knew she was making him feel good. She started out sucking him slowly and blowing on it. Then she gradually began to play with his balls as she sped up a little bit. He was growing bigger in her mouth and she loved being in control. This made her want to pleasure him more and she began to deep throat him. She made sure to wet it up and she was moaning so good that Nate knew that he wasn't going to last long. The feeling of him hitting the back of her throat was driving him wild. So to buy himself some time, he said, "Let's get on the bed."

She obliged and Nate spread her legs open and was so happy to see that she wasn't wearing any panties under her teddy. He put his head between her legs and started to tongue kiss her clit. She was instantly cumming. He loved to feel her shudder in his mouth. She was screaming loud enough for everyone in the hotel to hear her. Nate never broke his lock on her special place. After she climaxed, he continue to lick and suck on her determined to give her that same level of satisfaction again. Shauntel was still trying to catch her breath. He continued to lick and suck and soon she was swollen again. He started to rub on his member while continuing to pleasure her. She was getting jealous that he was having all of the fun. So she looked between his legs and asked him, "Why don't you come put that in my mouth?"

He did as he was asked and they continued to pleasure each other orally in the 69 position.

CHAPTER 8

Corey was the kind of guy that just attracted women. He was definitely easy on the eyes. He stood at 6 foot 2 inches with caramel brown smooth skin. He kept his hair cut in a well-manicured fade once a week with a naturally curly top. He shaved off all of his facial hair in order to maintain his boyish look. Most would consider him a pretty boy if he didn't have a physique that was perfectly chiseled. He was often mistaken for a professional basketball player and he had taken advantage of that with the ladies on many occasions. Even though he loved to score with the ladies, there was only one woman who had his heart. And he knew that he could never be with that one woman.

His son's mother Unique was more than fed up with his indiscretions. He had tried to plead his case to her that he was sorry for breaking her heart so many times. But to Unique it was like having a song you hated on repeat play. She had heard it all and was convinced that Corey would never change his ways. This last time that she caught him cheating on her was the last straw. They were not officially a couple at the time. But the night before, they'd had a three-hour heart to heart talk. Corey had admitted guilt to all of his infidelities and given her what seemed like a heartfelt apology before they spent all night getting busy. They never verbally agreed that they were going to try to work out their relationship. It was kind of implied though. So the next night, Unique took their son to her mother's house and decided to surprise him after work by going to his house so they could pick up where they had left off the night before. Only, she was the one surprised when she pulled up to his house and saw his truck rocking in the driveway. She walked up to the truck to see what was going on, but the windows were completely fogged up. So she snatched the driver's side back door opened and couldn't believe what she saw. Corey's ex-girlfriend Yvette's head flopped back while Corey was between her legs pounding her. Yvette screamed and tried to jump up, but she was caught off guard. And before she could sit up, Unique was punching her face like it was a punching bag. She got at least six good punches in before Corey was able to respond and push her off of Yvette. But while he was trying to restrain her, Unique started throw blows at him. She was screaming "You lying bastard. I can't believe that I actually believed you! You will never be able to tell the truth!" After taking a few punches, Corey was able to wrap his arms around the middle of her body with hers arms down. He picked her up and carried her to her car. She was squiggling, squirming and screaming the whole time. He opened her car door and sat her in the car seat. Before he closed her car door he said, "Stay right here, I've got to go make sure that girl doesn't need an ambulance."

Unique was pissed off. She waited a few seconds for him to get far enough from her for her to get to her trunk. She sprung out of the car and grabbed her steel bat out of the trunk, ran over to his Navigator and bust out the windshield with one swift swing. Corey was at

Yvette's car when he heard the sound of glass shattering. He ran to the front of his truck and saw his windshield busted but he didn't see Unique. "Unique you know that I don't believe in hitting women, but if you break another window, I swear I'm going to have to beat your ass." He heard the sound of the steel breaking glass again. Unique had just busted out his back window too. By this time, Yvette was walking up to Unique talking crazy trash about what she was going to do to her. Unique cocked the bat back. "Come on bitch! I can break your ass just like I'm breaking these windows!" Yvette kept walking towards Unique despite the fact that she was wielding a steel bat. Corey reached the back of the truck just as Unique swung the bat making contact with Yvette's chest. At the same time, Yvette sprayed Unique in the face with mace. Unique instantly dropped the bat and toppled over unaware of what had just happened. Yvette sprinted to her car and peeled out in excruciating pain. Unique had to flush her eyes with cold water for at least an hour before it wasn't burning anymore. That was the straw that broke the camel's back for her and she told Corey that night that it was over. She had told him that many times before. But he could tell by the look in her eyes that she actually meant it that night.

It had taken months to get Unique to even accept his phone calls. When she finally talked to him, she was really blunt. "Corey the only reason that I answered this phone is because I don't want to be the kind of mother that keeps her son from his father. But I have to love me more than I love any man! I have allowed you to break my heart over and over again. I refuse to ever let you hurt me again. So if you want to see your son, I won't stand in the way of that. But as for me and you, we will never be!" She hung up the phone. There was so much determination in her voice. Corey realized then that she was never going to forgive him. He felt really bad about what he had done to Unique, but it was just too hard for him to be monogamous at the time. Over the next few months, he did everything he could to make Unique reconsider. He never missed any of the scheduled visits with his son. He had always been a great dad, but he stepped his game up. He started taking her extra money outside of what he had already been giving Unique for his son, Corey Jr. He would take over expensive gifts for Unique and randomly send her flowers. He apologized to Unique every time he saw her and promised that he could be faithful if she would just give him another chance. But she wasn't budging. She was a different woman with a different look in her eye. If you looked at her long enough, you could tell that she had been scorned to the point of no return. Finally Corey accepted the fact that they would never be together as a couple and just focused on being a good father to his now 6-year-old son.

It had been about a year and Unique still hadn't started a new relationship with anyone. She didn't want to bring any new guys around her impressionable son. Besides, she and Corey were able to be cordial to each other for their son's sake. Corey caught her at a weak moment one night when he was bringing Corey Jr. back home. She hadn't had sex for over a year since the night before the fight and she was in desperate need of some hardcore sex. Corey sat down at the dining room table for some chitchat after they had put their son to bed. They talked about almost everything including the good times they had had in the past. The conversation started to become a little flirty and body temperatures started to rise. One thing led to another and before they knew it they were in Unique's bed having sex like two wild animals. Unique knew that she would never get back with Corey. But she had physical needs and he knew how to meet them. So every since then they had a friends with benefits type of relationship. Nobody's feelings were hurt because they were not committed to each other and their son had the luxury of being able to see his mom and dad together in the same house every now and then with no strife. So it was a win-win situation.

Corey worked at the Security Company with Nate during the day Monday through Friday and at Club Evolution Friday through Saturday nights. It was Monday and he had just finished his work on their newest contract and was preparing to lock up and go home when his cell phone rang. He looked at the caller ID and saw that it was Unique. He answered the call "What's up boo?"

"Nothing much. I was just wondering if we could move our date back by a few hours. Can you come at about 10 o'clock instead of 7 o'clock?"

"That's cool. I'm a little late wrapping things up at the office and I need to do some things before I come over anyway."

"Alright, I'll see you when you get here."

They disconnected the call. Corey locked up the office and set the burglar alarm. He got in his car and headed over to Nate's house to make sure that everything was in order there. He pulled to the back of the driveway and hopped out of the SUV. He walked around the house to make sure that nothing was wrong. Everything looked perfect so he hopped back in the car and called Nate to give him an update. Nate didn't answer the phone so he left a voicemail message letting him know that all was in order. Then he went to the bank and deposited all of the checks the security company had received from the week before. He merged onto the Chrysler freeway and headed to the gym to get a quick workout in. It was a good thing that Unique had asked him to postpone the time for a few hours. That gave him more time that he could spend in the gym working off frustrations. He worked out in the gym for about an hour and a half. Then he drove to a nearby walking track and jogged for about a half an hour. Satisfied with his workout, he headed home to take a shower before it was time for him to go to Unique's house. He took his shower and changed his clothes. He also grabbed his clothes for work for the next day. Whenever he ended up staying later for their rendezvous, Unique would let him stay over in the guest bedroom. It seemed like every since Unique had taken her heart back from him, she had become even more insatiable. The more he gave her, the more she wanted. He figured that it would be a very late night. Too late for him to plan to drive home afterwards.

****

He arrived at Unique's house a few minutes before 10 O'clock. He knocked on the door and she answered it fully dressed and wearing makeup. She was looking good too in her tight long sleeved black mini-dress. It was framing her curves perfectly. She was the epitome of 36-24-36. Unique was a plainly pretty girl who definitely didn't need any makeup and she hardly ever wore any. She also usually greeted him at the door wearing some sort of sexy lingerie or robe. He was a little thrown off with her being fully dressed. She hugged him and stepped back to let him in. They exchanged niceties. Then Corey made his way to his son's bedroom to tell him good night. His son was in the bed but he wasn't asleep yet. Corey could see him lying there with his eyes open from the light provided by the Elmo nightlight. He went over and kneeled next to the bed. "Hey daddy!"

"What's up little man?"

"Did mommy tell you what happened to me today?"

"No. What happened?"

"I got into a fight at school."

"What happened, CJ?"

"It's a girl name Destiny and she likes me and I like her. But Jacob likes her too. She don't like Jacob though."

Corey interrupted, "doesn't like Jacob."

"Oh Yeah. She doesn't like Jacob. So Jacob got mad because she wanted to hold my hand and not his. So he pushed me."

"And what did you do?"

"I told him not to push me again just like mommy told me to. But he didn't listen and he pushed me again. So I beat him up."

"Did you cry?"

"No but he did. I tried not to fight him, but he kept pushing me."

"Okay. It sounds like you did what you had to do. We will find out for sure when we go to the school to talk to the teacher. Don't worry about it. Daddy's got your back, okay?"

He gleamed up at Corey. "Okay Daddy."

"You have to be careful when dealing with little girls because if you're not they can get you into tons of trouble. That's a conversation for later though. I don't want you to worry about it. Just get some sleep and we will deal with it tomorrow. Okay?"

"Okay."

"Goodnight son."

"Goodnight Daddy."

No matter how scandalous of a life Corey led, he always felt redeemed by trying his best to mold his son into a good man. He was proud of Corey Jr. for standing up for himself and even prouder that he had won the fight.

When Corey was done talking to Corey Jr. he went in the living room to watch the News and waited for Unique to get out of the shower. He saw the report of Byron being executed. He thought to himself *'that dude looks familiar'*. He wasn't able to place where he had seen Byron before but he knew that he had seen him more than once before.

A few minutes later Unique pranced into the living room wearing a purple and black sheer teddy with black stilettos. Corey instantly rose to attention. No matter how many other women he had been with, Unique was the sexiest hands down. She had an innocent sexiness about her though. It was like she didn't mean to look that good, it just happened. They were quickly undressing each other and kissing all over each other's bodies. They moved their activities to the master bedroom a few minutes later and continued. Something seemed different about Unique. She was working it on him as usual. But she didn't really seem to be present in the moment. After their first round, she immediately went to take another shower. He was confused because normally they would just wait a few minutes and move on to round two. He lay in the bed flicking through the TV channels frustrated that there was never anything good to watch on TV anymore. Unique walked back in after her shower brushing her long black Remy hair.

"Unique is everything okay?"

She was wrapping her hair up into a scarf. "Yeah. Everything is fine. You can stay over if you want to in the guestroom but I need to go to sleep now."

"Really?"

"Really. I have to get up early."

"You always have to get up early. That has never stopped you from giving it to me for a few hours before."

"I know. I'm just tired Corey. Can you turn the light off on your way out?"

He couldn't believe his ears. Normally she would wear him out until mid-morning. Now it felt like she was basically putting him out of the room. He accepted that for now and went into the guestroom. His anticipation kept him awake. He had really been looking forward to the normal strenuous activity they shared. He couldn't sleep. He just lay on his back and stared at the ceiling wrecking his brain for an explanation for this new Unique. He decided that he would have some solo fun to take his mind off of it.

****

The next morning Corey and Unique went to his son's school to meet with the principal. The meeting went pretty smooth. The principal let them both know that Jacob had been trouble every since he started attending the school. The principal let Corey Jr. off with a stern warning that violence would not be tolerated. She promised Corey and Unique that she would be contacting them with a date for a follow up conference with Jacob's mother.

Corey turned down the street that the Security Company was on and was unable to go any further.

The police had the whole street blocked off and there were so many gawkers on the street that he wasn't able to see what was going on. He waved over a police officer.

"Excuse me Officer, what is happening up there? I'm trying to get to work."

"There was an explosion up ahead at one of the businesses in the middle of the block. We cannot allow any cars through here."

"So how am I supposed to get to my office?"

"You are going to have to park somewhere else for now. You will just need to show your ID to the officers at the perimeter and they will let you walk to your office."

Corey backed off of the street and went around the block and parked on the next street over. He walked back around the corner and approached the yellow tape at the perimeter of the scene with his Security ID out and ready to show. The officer looked at his ID.

"You work for Network Security?"

"Yes. I am the manager."

"Where is the owner?"

"He is out of town right now so I am in charge."

"Okay buddy. There was an incident at your office a few hours ago. We have been trying to contact your boss but have been unsuccessful."

"What do you mean an incident?"

"Follow me."

Corey didn't like the feeling he had. But he did as he was told and followed the officer. When he got a couple of buildings down from the Security Company, he noticed that something was missing.

He saw a part of the sky that he had never been able to see because of the buildings downtown. He kept walking and soon saw that the Security Company was almost non-existent. It looked like the whole top half of it had been blown off. There was debris everywhere. He looked at the officer. "What the hell happened?"

"Sir I'm taking you to the captain so that he can explain."

****

Nate and Shauntel were basking in the pleasure of their explosive labor. He leaned over and kissed her on the cheek. "Nate I'm tired of being in this bed. There has to be something I can do that won't be too strenuous without having to stay in this room. I'm going stir crazy."

"It's a good thing you said that. We are on the same page baby. I picked up something I thought you might like while I was out." He got out of the bed and walked into the living room of the suite. He came back and handed her a brochure while he was climbing back in bed. She looked at the cover. "An indoor beach?"

He smiled from ear to ear. He knew she would love it. "Yep."

She was thumbing through the pamphlet amazed. "Oh my God, Nate. This is so awesome. I wonder who thought of this."

"I don't know but that brochure really is not a good representation. I went over to see it in person. I couldn't believe somebody was smart enough to create something that banging."

"I want to go!"

"I figured you would. We can go right after we eat and shower if you want to."

She laid her head on his chest and rubbed his six pack. "Nate while you were out getting the food, I saw a news report online and Byron was killed execution style."

Nate seemed unsurprised. "Really?"

She lifted her head and looked him in the eye. "Did you have anything to do with that?"

"What makes you think that Tel?"

"I'm not sure what to think. That's why I'm asking you."

"Tel I know we agreed to be honest with each other. Some things don't even need to be talked about though."

While she was thinking of how to pose the next question, Nate's phone rang Big Punisher's, "Off With His Head". 'Saved by the bell', he thought. He snapped the phone open. "What's up Corey?"

"We've got a situation."

"What now?"

"There was an explosion at the office. The police are saying that it was bombed."

Nate's voice raised about ten octaves. "What?"

"I know man. They said that the burglar alarm went off about ten minutes before the explosion. The police were pulling up just as the explosion went off. "

"Oh shit! I'm going to have to cut the vacation short and come back now!"

"Naw man. Don't worry about it. I've got it. You'll be back tomorrow night anyway right?"

"Yeah but I need to be there now."

"No you don't. You don't trust me?" "Now you know if it's any dude that I trust, it's you."

"Okay then. Let me handle it. There's really nothing you can do right now except answer the police's questions and I can do that. I already told them that you were out of town and they are preparing to interview me now."

"Alright man. Have you checked on the house?"

"Not since last night. But I'll go check again just to make sure when I'm done over here."

"Okay. Call me if anything else happens. And please keep your phone on so that I can get in touch with you. You know how you do."

"Naw man you don't have to worry about that. I told you I've got this one. I know how serious this is."

"Alright." Before they disconnected the call Nate said "Corey?"

"Yeah."

There was a brief pause. "Thanks man."

"For sure."

Shauntel hurriedly asked, "What's wrong?"

Nate was shaking his head back and forth. "Somebody bombed the office."

****

Nate was absolutely right about the pictures in the brochure not doing the indoor beach any justice. It was breathtaking and it had the genuine feel of being on a real beach. From the blues on the wall and the real sand which bordered the man made Ocean with the sound of the crashing waves to the glass ceiling that slid open for the sun to beam in, everything was just as it needed to be for beach lovers. The heating and cooling was set up so that every few minutes you would feel a warm breeze no matter what time of year it was. There were beach chairs and tables adorned with sunbrellas. The four palm trees that were strategically placed in each corner of the huge room were at least 7 feet tall. Shauntel was beyond pleased with this trip. She was stretched out on a beach lounge chair breathing in the beautiful air next to the man of her dreams.

"Nate we need to figure out a date for the wedding. I don't know if we should wait until after I have the baby or if we should do this in the next couple of months. All I know for sure is that I don't want to have to wear a maternity wedding dress."

"You know what I say. Never put off until tomorrow what you can do today."

"We also have to consider the fact that they are trying to send me to prison."

"Tel you are not going to prison. I promise you that!"

"I'm glad that you are so sure, because I'm not."

"Trust me."

"So you think we should do this before I start showing?"

"Yes. Is that enough time for you to plan it?"

"Don't you know I'm superwoman?"

"You sure are; only sexier." He leaned over and kissed her.

Through her blushing, she told him, "I'm only kidding but with Tasha's skills in event planning and my extra time having to lie in bed, I'm sure we can pull it off in the next couple of months."

Nate pulled out his cell phone and opened his calendar application. "Okay, April twenty-first is almost exactly eight weeks away and it's on a Saturday."

"That was my Grandmother's birthday. That would be perfect. We can do it in her honor since she won't be able to be there."

"Great. You just tell me what you need me to do and we can make it happen."

"Okay we need to set a color scheme so that I can get started. That is the most important decision to make first because that is the determining factor for everything."

"That is totally up to you. I'm with anything you pick as long as it's not something crazy like red and green."

She playfully punched him in his arm. "You know I wouldn't pick anything crazy like that. I've got a good idea. We should stop on our way home and pick up some bridal books for me to look through to get some ideas."

"You've got it babe. Now I *have* to get in that water to see if it feels as much like the ocean as it looks."

He ran and jumped in the water. It was nice and cool just like ocean water. He swam for at least 30 minutes while Shauntel relaxed in the chair and took a light nap. Afterwards they acted like kids. They buried their feet in the sand and wrote their love for each other in the sand. Neither of them had had so much fun since they were actually kids.

CHAPTER 9

Shauntel was getting homesick before her and Nate left Illinois. But to come home to more drama made her wish she had extended the trip some. When they got home and got out of the truck there was such a horrible smell that they had to hold their breath. They soon found out that somebody had put manure all over Nate's lawn and all around the condo. The smell was so extreme that Shauntel had lit every scented candle when she got inside to try to counter the smell. It was three hours later and the candles were finally starting to work. Nate had called a cleaning crew to come clean it up as soon as he got in the house and they were just finishing up outside. There was also a note taped to the door and it was typed. It read:

"This can all be over if you just give me what's rightfully mine. My woman!"

The videotape from the surveillance system showed that the manure was put down two days before they came home, the same night the office had been blown up. They had reviewed the surveillance tape over and over again trying to figure out who in the world would do something as nasty as put manure everywhere. The person was dressed in all black including a black baseball cap though. That made it extremely hard to see his face. He was smart enough to keep his head down at all times too. The perpetrator was always just a little bit outside of the full camera frame. You could tell that the guy was stocky. Aside from that, they had no clue what he looked like or who it could be. Shauntel was so tired of the mystery of it all. With Byron being dead, who could be the stalker? Tasha had just arrived and they were sitting on the living room sectional getting ready to get caught up.

"Tasha, I'm sorry about that smell. We just had another incident."

"What smell?"

"You don't smell that?"

"Now that you mentioned it, I do smell a hint of something not nice. I did smell it outside, but I assumed somebody got a little heavy handed while doing their garden. Other than that all I could smell were those million candles you're burning."

Shauntel laughed. Her laugh quickly turned into a cry.

"Shauntel,   what's   wrong?"
"I'm just tired of all of this craziness. Every time I turn around there is something else going on. I don't have time to catch my breath."

"I'm sorry Shauntel. What happened now?"

She pointed the remote toward the TV and muted the volume.

"When Nate and I got home there was manure everywhere. That is what that cleaning crew is out there doing. The smell was so foul that I had to light all of these candles. It took forever to get that smell out of my nose. I'm sure that you heard what happened at Nate's office on the news. It's just too much."

"I haven't been watching the news. It is too depressing. What happened at Nate's office?"

"The same night of the manure incident somebody blew up his office."

"What the hell? Did the police catch who did it?"

"I'm not sure yet. Nate is going to go see Corey as soon as the cleaning crew is done outside."

"I hope they caught whoever did it."

"Me too. Tasha, I'm sorry. I know that something is going on with you and here I am taking over the conversation with my drama. I think my hormones have a lot to do with it too." She wiped her tears. "I will be okay. Now tell me what is going on with you."

Shauntel saw Tasha's discomfort with the question in her body language as she shifted on the sofa.

"I'm going to tell you everything. Before I do though, I thought that Byron was dead?"

"He is and now I am totally confused about who could be doing all of this crazy stuff."

Tasha rethought her earlier decision not to tell Shauntel about her having Junior to vandalize her house. She decided that she still wouldn't tell her for now. It would be better to wait it out and make sure that Junior could be a threat first. Tasha exhaled loudly.

"Shauntel, do you remember Junior?"

"Junior from high school?"

"Yeah."

"I remember him. What about him?"

"You know that he is a hustler. Well I asked him to do something for me that I really regret now. I promised him that I would go on a date with him if he did it for me."

"What?"

"Yeah, but I wasn't serious though. When he figured out that I was not going to go out with him, he got mad."

Now Tasha's tears were flowing. "Shauntel, he attacked me and raped me."

Shauntel was shocked and she didn't know what to say as she watched Tasha drop her face into her hands. Her crying was audible. Shauntel walked over to Tasha and sat beside her. She wrapped her arm around her friends back and rocked her. "Oh my God, Tasha I am so sorry. You should have told me. I would have come straight home."

"I didn't want to ruin your vacation."

"I can always go on a vacation. You should not have had to go through this by yourself."

"I know but I really didn't have to go through it by myself. I met a rape counselor and she was there with me every step of the way. She even went to the hospital with me and stayed with me while I had to take the rape examination. It was horrible."

"Are you okay?"

"I will be. It will be a long journey, but the counselor has really helped me out a lot. I am going to be seeing her on a regular basis. I'm just so mad at myself for putting myself in a position for something like this to happen."

"Tasha, you know that you can't blame this on yourself. He is the asshole who is wrong. You did nothing wrong! I am going to kill him!"

"Well he is in jail and probably won't be getting out anytime soon, so that will be hard."

"Good. He needs to be castrated and hung to death."

Tasha nodded her head slowly in agreement. "I don't want to dwell on the negative Shauntel. Can we please talk about something positive now?"

They were both wiping their tears away. Shauntel exhaled loudly, "Yes. Nate wants to have this wedding in two months and I know that you can make it the best wedding in the history of weddings. But will it be too much for you to be my maid of honor and help with the planning?"

"Of course not. Now that is the kind of positivity I need." Tasha picked up one of the wedding magazines. "Have you picked your colors yet?"

"Not yet. I really am not sure what will work for me. My favorite color is purple and Nate's is blue. He doesn't really care what colors I choose so I would just go with purple if I wasn't afraid of it turning out looking like an episode of Barney."

"Girl you are too crazy. It won't look like Barney. Purple is royalty and we can make it look like royalty. Have you thought about a venue yet?"

"No. I figured we could brainstorm and come up with a few choices."

"Okay. Where is your laptop so that we can do that now?"

"It's on the kitchen counter."

Tasha grabbed the laptop and immediately started pulling up information on the different venues she had in mind for the wedding.

"Tasha, I am scared that Nate may have had something to do with the Byron thing."

Tasha was whispering. "You think he had Byron killed?"

"I'm not sure. But, when I asked him about it, he didn't deny it."

They heard Nate coming through the side door. Tasha was quick on her feet. "Shauntel I think purple would be a great color. I can make that look really elegant."

Nate walked into the living room. "It's all done. I'm going to take a shower so that I can go holla at Corey. Holla if you need me."

Shauntel looked so innocent. "Okay baby."

The girls got busy with their plans and scheduled everything around Shauntel's bed rest situation. By the time they were finished three hours later, they had scheduled for Shauntel's stylist to come over with 20 different gowns for her to try on in the styles that she liked. They also had a cake tasting scheduled for the following week. Tasha promised to bring over pictures of the three best venues she had in mind the next day. They had also picked out the bridesmaids dresses from a combination of two dresses at a local bridal store's website. They planned to show those dresses to the stylist and have her create the perfect dresses. Shauntel called her cousin Erica and her friend Harmony and they were both excited to agree to be bridesmaids. Tasha told Shauntel that she would pick up the decorations from the warehouse she always used and bring them over in a few days for her approval. Shauntel told her that there was no need for her to approve the decorations because she had seen her work and totally trusted her to make it perfect. They were exhausted.

Nate had left to go meet with Corey and they were ready to unwind. Tasha went to the kitchen and poured her a glass of wine and Shauntel a glass of sparkling cider. She brought back a light snack and they both got comfortable in the sectional recliners and started to chat. Shauntel looked at Tasha. "So, somebody has a birthday coming up."

"You know, I haven't even thought about it with all of the depressing stuff that's going on around me. But this wedding is just what I needed to lift my spirits. Thanks girl."

"You don't have to thank me. There is no way I'm going to let you slip into a depression. We are going to plan you the flyest party ever planned. I am going to be here with you through all of the bull too."

Tasha smiled. It was nice to see her smile. It was like she had a permanent frown since she had gotten to the condo. "Shauntel I don't know about a party."

"Well I do. Girl you are turning the big 3-0. It is a must to have a party for that!"

"Okay. What do you have in mind?"

"I don't know. Aren't you the *party planner*?" They both laughed.

"I am the *party planner*, but I don't know what to do."

"I was just joking. I've got you. We're going to throw you a huge party at Club Evolution. I'll even order some male strippers if you want."

"That sounds good but I don't think Nate is going for that one. We might be able to pull that off for your bachelorette party. That's what we forgot to plan."

"I'm not worried about that now. We can talk about that later. I don't want to think about the wedding anymore today. It's giving me a headache just talking about it."

"Okay so we can have a party at Club Evolution."

"We will have Nate reserve us a VIP section. We need a theme though."

Just then, Shauntel saw Byron's picture flash across the Television screen. She quickly grabbed the remote and turned the mute off.

"In a twisted turn of events, a man may have gotten himself killed in his selfish attempt at criminal activity. This man Byron Stewart has been believed to be dead for four days. It turns out that Byron

Stewart is alive and well and was unaware that he was presumed dead until he saw the news report informing him that he had been killed execution style. Police say that the man believed to be Mr. Stewart bore a significant resemblance to Mr. Stewart and they are in the process of determining his identity. Mr. Stewart re-located from Detroit Michigan to Atlanta Georgia just a couple of months ago. He called the police to get to the bottom of the news report. That is when police discovered that this mystery man was in fact not Byron Stewart and had stolen Mr. Stewart's identity and eased right into living his lifestyle. Including living in Mr. Stewart's home, using credit cards in his name and even purchasing and driving an SUV registered to Mr. Stewart. Mr. Stewart's shock was apparent in this interview."

The screen jumped to an interview of Byron.

"I was watching the internet news when I saw a report with my name on it. I clicked on it and the news lady was saying that I had been killed. I was

like 'what the hell'. So I called the police to see what was going on."

The camera flashed back to the news reporter.

"As you've just seen Mr. Stewart's shock is apparent. Police have taken fingerprints from the deceased and are waiting for results to determine who the mystery man is. We will keep you posted on this story as updates come in."

Shauntel and Tasha were staring at each other in shock. Neither of them knew what to say. Shauntel's expression looked more like fear than shocked though.

****

Corey met Nate at the Club Evolution where they both worked as bouncers on the weekends. Nate was the head of security with Corey as his backup in case he was ever not able to be there. They were the perfect team because they could read each other's faces because of their long history and they were both very observant of their surroundings. They had always been able to control any altercations because of those two things. They were both sitting at the bar having a beer. Corey was giving Nate an update of the events. "I can't believe how incompetent these police are. It's like they all dropped out of school in kindergarten. They are telling me that the bomb went off right as a patrol car was pulling up in response to the alarm going off and that the surveillance system was completely destroyed. I asked them about satellite surveillance and they looked at me like I was speaking a foreign language. They hammered me with questions like I was the one who did it. So prepare yourself to get the same treatment."

"Do they have any leads?"

"They wouldn't tell me that. All they did was keep asking me the same questions over and over again. I guess they were hoping that I was lying and would slip up and forget what I said before. Once they saw that my story was never going to change after four hours, they gave me that BS about they would be in touch."

Nate shook his head back and forth and wiped the sweat from his forehead. "This shit is driving me crazy. I'm not used to not being able to fix a situation."

"I understand man. I went by the house to make sure that everything was okay when they finally released me and everything looked like it was all good."

"You must not have gotten out of the car?"

"No. I didn't because I was just over there looking around the night before and everything was fine. I didn't see anything wrong from inside the car so I bounced. Don't tell me something else happened."

"Some asshole put manure everywhere around the house. The smell is indescribable."

"Manure?"

"Yes. Animal shit! The smell was so loud that I smelled it before I even got out of the car. You didn't smell it?"

"Naw man. I didn't smell anything. My head was so messed up from all of that interrogating though. I might have just blocked it out."

"Corey I need you to keep your head in the game. I got rid of both of the people that could have been doing this and it's still going on. I have no clue where to even look next."

"We need to start with you and Shauntel's enemies."

"If I have any enemies, I don't know who they are and the only enemies I could see Shauntel having would be an ex of hers."

Nate looked like he had a fresh idea. "Wait a minute."

"What's up?"

"Shauntel's best friend Tasha told me that she had been harboring some bad feelings toward Shauntel for a long time and that she had recently worked it out."

"You think she could be doing it?"

"I'm not sure. She could've had somebody else to do all of this shit. I'll tell you what; I'll hook you up with her so that you can go out with her for a while to get in her head. Maybe you can milk her for some information and find out if she has anything to do with it."

"I don't know about that one Nate. You remember what happened the last time I played with a girl's heart."

"I do. You ended up being able to tap that at your convenience, no strings attached."

"That *was* the case. Unique has been acting real brand new lately, like she don't want to be bothered."

"What do you think that's about?"

"I'm not sure but I intend to find out."

"Look Corey. I'm not asking you to marry the girl. You don't even have to sleep with her. All I'm asking you to do is just take her on a couple of dates. Make her feel like she's Beyoncé or somebody. Get her drunk so that she will get to spilling her secrets. Okay?"

Corey was reluctant. "Okay. I'm going to get up outta here. It's my day to go 'tap that' as you say."

"Have fun."

Corey paid the bartender and left for Unique's house. He wasn't sure what to expect when he got there because she had been acting really distant lately. Even though they had scheduled to have their meeting a couple of days ago, he hadn't talked to her since then and she wasn't answering her phone or responding to his text messages.

He pulled up to Unique's house and noticed that her car wasn't there. He went to the door and knocked anyway. There was no answer. He got back into his car and called her. She didn't answer her phone. He really wasn't in the mood for Unique's games. He was actually only concerned with seeing his son. He called Unique's mother and asked her if Unique was there.

She told him that she hadn't come to pick up Corey Jr. yet. He asked to speak to his son. He had a short conversation with Corey Jr. letting him know that he loved him and would see him soon. After he disconnected the call, he sat in Unique's driveway contemplating on calling her again and leaving a voicemail message. He finally convinced himself that the best way to make her come to him was not to chase her. He sent her a text message instead. *"I was here for our date and you were not. Holla at yo boy."*

He pulled out of the driveway with no destination in mind.

CHAPTER 10

Shauntel's four weeks were officially over and she was feeling really nervous about what the doctor might say. She had been following the emergency room doctor's orders to the best of her ability. She and Nate hadn't had any sex since the 69 pleasures they'd shared on their vacation. She barely ever got out of the bed because Nate or Tasha was always there making sure that she had everything she needed. She was ready to get back to normal and get some of her man! She was really anxious because Tasha's birthday party was scheduled for the next night and they had really planned the perfect 30th birthday celebration at the club. She needed the all clear so that she could go over to the club the next day and help the party planner with the decorations. She wanted everything to be perfect for Tasha so that her spirits would really be lifted. She seemed as if the planning the wedding had really helped bring her out of her funk. But, Shauntel really wanted to do something nice for her in return.

Nate was really nervous. He didn't do well with doctors and hospitals. He was so excited that he was going to have a little boy to carry on his name and it had been very hard to keep that secret from Shauntel. He respected her wishes to not want to know though. To avoid her finding out from anybody else he made sure not to tell anybody and that was what was really making it hard. The nurse came out of the office door and called Shauntel to the back. When she stood up, her knees were knocking. She really just wanted everything to be perfect. The first thing the nurse wanted her to do was to stand on the scale. Her weight was 5lbs less than when she got pregnant. She looked at the nurse worriedly. "I lost five pounds. Shouldn't I be gaining weight?"

"Actually it's pretty common for women to lose weight in their first trimester of pregnancy. The morning sickness makes them eat less. Have you been nauseous or throwing up?"

"Both."

"That's normal. It's nothing to worry about as long as you have been eating right. The nausea is a good sign. It means the baby is developing properly."

"I have been trying to eat right, but most times I don't have an appetite."

"I don't think it's anything to worry about. You can talk to the doctor more about it when you see her. Follow me."

The nurse led Nate and Shauntel down the narrow hallway to a door with a number 4 marked on it. They followed her into the room. The nurse took Shauntel's blood pressure, temperature and pulse rate all the while jotting down all of the results in her chart. "Ms. Barnes, I will need you to get completely undressed and put on this gown. You can put your clothes in the under bed storage and get comfortable. The doctor will be in shortly."

Shauntel had been seeing the same OB/GYN since she was sixteen years old. Her name was Dr. Coleman. She had a great bedside manner and was very personable. If a patient ran into her outside of the office she was always cordial and she knew all of her patients by name. Shauntel got undressed and put on the gown that the nurse had left for her. Nate folded and put her clothes in the drawer underneath the bed. He sat in the chair next to the exam bed. Shauntel was instantly cold and the smells from the medicine in the office were making her nauseous. There was a light knock on the door and the doctor entered the room holding Shauntel's medical chart.

"Well hello Shauntel."

"Hey Dr. Coleman."

"So I hear that we're having a baby."

Shauntel nodded her head. "Yes we are."

Dr. Coleman looked at Nate and extended her hand for him to shake. "Hi. I'm Dr. Coleman."

Nate shook her hand. "Nice to meet you. I'm Nate."

The doctor looked back at Shauntel.

"Dr. Coleman this is my fiancé and the one who is responsible for us having a baby."

"Well congratulations you too. How are you feeling?"

"I'm feeling really good except for the nausea."

"That's good. I can help you with the nausea. Keep you something minty around at all times. It really helps. Crackers are another really good help for nausea. Just don't eat too many crackers. Have you had any bleeding or spotting since your emergency room visit?"

"No."

"Any pain?"

"No."

"Great. Now I will need to do a pelvic exam, a quick ultrasound and take a little blood. I'm going to go get the nurse for assistance. I'll be right back."

Shauntel looked at Nate's face and he looked distressed. "Are you okay baby?"

"I'm good. I think I'm going to step out while they do the exam. Are you okay?"

"I'm fine, but you look like you're about to pass out."

"I'm good."

He kissed her on the cheek and started to walk out of the room. She started to make fun of him. "You big chicken." She started making chicken noises. "Bock bock bock."

"I'm not chicken but all of that blood and pelvis talk is too much for me. I'll see you in a minute."

Shauntel made it through her exams with flying colors. Dr. Coleman gave her another prescription for prenatal vitamins and released her from bed rest with a stern warning. "If you have any symptoms that are unusual make sure you call me immediately. You still have my cell number right?"

"Yep. I have you on speed dial."

"Okay. Make an appointment for 8 weeks from today with the receptionist on your way out and you're free to go. You take care of yourself and I will be looking for my wedding invitation."

Shauntel was amped. She was officially off of bed rest and was excited about going to do some normal activities for a change.

****

Tasha was sitting in the lobby of the counselor's office waiting to see her psychologist. As she looked around, she took note of the patients that were in the lobby. She had a better understanding of why people didn't want to go to a therapist a lot of times. One woman was in the corner having a conversation all by herself like she was two people. Her hair was all over her head and she was wearing mismatched shoes. Every time one of the personalities would speak she would turn her head. For the ten minutes that Tasha had been sitting there, she had figured out that one of the personalities was named Marcia and the other was named Beverly. In the most recent conversation, Marcia was mad at Beverly because Beverly told

Marcia that her shoes didn't match. The lady whipped her head to the left in Tasha's direction. "You shut up Beverly. You don't know nothing 'bout fashion no way. I'm the one who was the model til that bitch Tyra stole my man who was the president of the modeling agency and he gave her my contract." She whirled her head around to the right. "You shut up Marcia. You know damn well that you ain't never been no model. How you gone be a model with that big ass stomach?"

She jerked her head back to the left. "Beverly I know you not talking about nobody's stomach when you got that big ole She-nay-nay booty. I can see yo cellulite through your pants."

Tasha was trying her best to tune the conversation out, but it was hard because the lady was loud. She wondered why nobody else in the office was looking at the lady like she was crazy. Looking at them though, they all looked like they were in their own little world. The white man who was sitting directly across from her looked especially self-engulfed. He looked like he was going bald naturally. But every few seconds he would reach into his hair, do a scratching motion and snatch out a hair. There was only one other person in the lobby who looked like she didn't belong there. She was well put together almost too put together. She looked to be in her early fifties.

Not a hair was out of place. Every so often she would squirm in her chair, clear her throat and tug on her cardigan sweater exactly in that order.

Beverly was getting louder in the corner. "Bitch don't make me whip your ass up in here. You remember what happened the last time I had to whip your ass." The lady snatched her head to the left and closed her eyes. "Ain't nobody scared of yo ass Beverly. Don't get shit twisted. I've been taking karate. "She slowly turned her head to the right, put her hand on her hip and rolled her neck. "Marcia you always lying. You don't know nothing about no karate."

A counselor came into the lobby. "Ilene?" The lady stopped arguing with herself and blinked her eyes really hard and fast over and over. Then she got up and walked toward the counselor and followed her to the back.

It took everything in Tasha not to get up and walk out of there. She didn't want to be labeled. But she knew she really needed to talk to somebody who didn't really know her. Her issues ran deep all the way back to her childhood. Finally, April walked into the lobby and called Tasha to the back. April made sure Tasha was comfortable before she started asking questions. "Is there anything in particular you would like to talk about today Tasha?"

Tasha shrugged her shoulders. "Not really."

"Okay well why don't we start from the beginning? Give me an overview of your life since childhood."

Tasha told April about how the only happy memories she had of her childhood were the earliest ones. That was before she was old enough to understand that her mother was a drug addict who had no idea who Tasha's father was. Her mother was always tricking and bringing random men in and out of their house. Many of those men had taken advantage of Tasha by rubbing up against her or touching in the wrong place. A couple of them had actually made her touch them. She was lucky in that none of them had actually ever penetrated her. But that gave her an early disdain for the male species. She felt like they were all dogs. Her early development further confirmed her feelings about guys. All of the boys in school were trying to get her goodies. It eventually got to the point that Tasha's mother was hardly ever home. Tasha had mixed feelings about that. She was happy that her mother wasn't there so that she wouldn't have to help her get high or worry about the tricks trying to molest her. On the other hand, she was desperately in need of a love from her mother that she was unequipped to give her. Finally, in fifth grade, she met Shauntel and they instantly clicked. They became best friends within a week. She started hanging out at Shauntel's house so that she wouldn't have to see her mother most of the time. Plus Shauntel's grandmother cooked the best food in town and Tasha was lucky if her mother cooked once a week. She told her about her mother dying from an overdose and how none of the family ever showed any interest in her. She let her know that Shauntel's family was the only family that she had ever really had. Shauntel's grandmother had raised her from the time she was 15 and Shauntel was like a sister to her. That was until Shauntel went to the prom with the only guy Tasha had ever liked. She had the biggest crush on Dominic Shrivers. He was a wide receiver on the High School football team. All the girls used to throw themselves at him and he never flirted back with them. He was tall, fair skinned with naturally curly hair. He was the cutest boy in school. It didn't hurt that he was a Christian boy with old school ways. He never gawked at Tasha like the other boys and he was always polite. She had been so closed off to the opposite sex though. She didn't know how to let him know that she had a huge crush on him. Shauntel on the other hand knew exactly how to let him know that she liked him and he asked her to the prom. Tasha was completely crushed. Once again, she felt that the person she needed had betrayed her. From that day she began to develop envy for Shauntel even though she never told Shauntel how she felt about

Dominic either. The envy reached its peak when Dominic bought Shauntel a beautiful diamond necklace on graduation day. She went on to tell the doctor how she had only had 3 real romantic relationships in her adulthood. She sabotaged each of those relationships when she felt that the guys were getting too close to her. She threw herself into her event planning business so that she wouldn't have to think about it. It had been years since she had been in a committed relationship because she felt like it was just a waste of her time. She told her about the recent experience at church that helped her change the feelings that she'd had toward Shauntel. She had begun to feel good about herself finally and wanted her and Shauntel's friendship to go back to what it was before the prom. She was also considering opening herself up to a romantic relationship. The rape had been a major setback though and she felt herself slipping into a depression and building walls again. She ended the long story with, "so here I am today."

"Thank you for explaining all of that to me Tasha. That really shed a lot of light on what is going on and the kind of plan you and I can create to help you take back control of your life. You have been through a lot. The good news is that you can make a conscious decision today to deal with these issues, which will help to improve your quality of life. I have a few questions for you. Did the rape bring to mind any of the abuse you experienced in your childhood?"

"It felt like I was going through all of it all over again."

"What exactly did that feel like?"

"I felt my mother abandoning me. I felt all of those men touching me inappropriately. I felt my family turn their backs on me. I felt the only person I ever trusted betray me."

"What did you feel emotionally?"

"I felt guilty, betrayed, alone and afraid."

"Those are genuine feelings. Do you know why you felt guilty?"

"I just felt like if I would have never lied to him, he would have never done that to me."

"Do you still feel like that?"

"Sometimes I do. My conscious knows that he was the one in the wrong, not me. My subconscious feels that it's partly my fault."

"How are you sleeping Tasha?"

"Not good."

"When you say not good, does that mean you can't get to sleep or you have trouble staying sleep?"

"I have trouble going to sleep and I wake up from nightmares almost every night."

"Have you always had issues sleeping?"

"On and off for most of my life I have."

April paused for about a minute to give Tasha some time. "Okay it sounds like there are a few things going on. Firstly, it sounds like we are dealing with some serious abandonment issues. That is to be expected with all that you have experienced. Abandoned Child Syndrome usually begins at an early age. What usually happens is that children feel abandoned at a young age and so they begin to assume that everyone will abandon them. In order to avoid the pain that accompanies that abandonment, they begin to close themselves off emotionally. The things you have experienced are the types of things that can cause this. Some of the feelings you described are symptoms of the syndrome. So are the sleeping issues and some other things. It is not a disorder like some of the other things that are going on and we can easily work out a plan to reverse this."

"Is the plan going to include medication? I don't want to take any mind altering drugs."

"I believe in trying to heal people through communication and exercises. I am not quick to put any of my patients on medicine unless I feel it is absolutely necessary. I believe in your case we should be able to get you back on track without any medication."

Tasha breathed out loudly. "Thank goodness. I hate taking medicine."

"So do I Tasha. Sometimes it's necessary though. I think you will be fine without it. Now have you ever heard of PTSD?"

"Sounds familiar. What's that?"

"It's an acronym for Post Traumatic Stress Disorder. This one is not as straightforward because it can stem from multiple traumas. I need you to think back to the rape. Were you feeling like "here we go again"?"

"Absolutely."

"And did this incident seem to rehash the past abuse you experienced?"

"Definitely."

"Do you find yourself feeling detached from life or not really interested in things you were interested in before?"

"All of the time."

She handed Tasha a packet of information. "Tasha I am going to give you this workbook for PTSD. I would like for you to take some time over the next two weeks to complete this and please be totally honest. When you come back in two weeks, we will be able to review your answers and decide how severe the PTSD is and develop a treatment plan. Also, I want you to try your best to follow this meal and exercise plan as close as possible to try to combat the Abandoned Child Syndrome symptoms."

Tasha took the packet. "Wow this seems like a lot."

"I know it does. It's really not and you have two weeks to get used to this. It's like eating an elephant, one bite at a time." She gave Tasha a friendly smile.

Tasha dropped her head. "I guess my problem is that I like to try to eat the whole elephant all at once."

"It's a learned process my dear. And the more you focus on healing the faster you will be back to your normal self. Make an appointment for two weeks from today with the receptionist on your way out."

"Okay. See you then doc."

****

Corey wasn't sure what exactly was going on with Unique lately, but he knew something was wrong. It had been over two weeks since they had seen each other and she had been really standoffish during the 2 brief conversations they did have then. It was their night to see each other. He stopped by the flower shop and picked her up 2-dozen premium red roses. He also bought her a friendship card that perfectly expressed how grateful he felt about her remaining friends with him and allowing him to have a relationship with his son. He thought about buying her some jewelry, but he didn't want to overstep his boundaries. He really just wanted to know why she had been treating him so differently all of a sudden and what he could do to fix it.

As he walked up to her door, he made up his mind that he was not leaving without an explanation. Unique opened the door so quick that she had to be standing at the door waiting for him. She was wearing a headscarf and a terry cloth robe. He stepped in and handed her the gift bag with the flowers and greeting card and gave her a peck on the cheek. Her body language screamed that she did not want to be touched. He decided to ignore that until after he was able to spend some time Corey Jr.

"Thanks for the flowers."

Corey was looking around for Corey Jr. "You're welcome. Where's CJ?"

"He's not here. I took him over to my mom's house so that we could talk."

They both sat down on the sofa. "What's wrong Unique?"

"I really don't know how to tell you this other than to just come right out and say it."

Corey was looking her dead in her eye but she was looking past him.

"Corey, we can't do this anymore."

He looked confused. "Do what?"

"See each other romantically."

He felt a knot in his throat. He knew that it might take some time but he thought that eventually he and Unique would be able to move forward and he could really have his family together. "What do you mean?" What did I do wrong?"

"It's not your fault Corey. I've been seeing someone and it is getting serious. We have decided to be exclusive."

Corey knew that things had been different, but he definitely did not see this coming. He was at a loss for words.

"Corey I know that I have been MIA a lot lately. That is because I was spending time with him; trying to give you space and honestly I didn't know how to tell you."

He was trying to absorb all that she was telling him. "What do you mean giving me space? I was trying to close the gap between us."

Unique shifted in her seat. "We both knew what this was Corey. We were two grown people fulfilling each other's sexual needs. Outside of that, we could never move further because of our past."

His expression was turning into a frown of a reflection of what he was feeling inside, anger. "Who is this dude anyway?"

Unique stood up and her discomfort showed in her posture. "He's just a guy I met at work last month."

Corey stood up now and faced her. "Just a guy, huh? I know you are not planning to bring just a guy around my son."

Unique put her hands on her hips and rolled her head back in exhaustion. "See Corey this is just why I didn't want to tell you about this because I knew that you would start tripping."

"You damn right I'm tripping. You know that I don't play when it comes to my son."

"This has nothing to do with CJ, Corey. I would never bring some random guy around him and you know it. You are standing here talking about you don't play when it comes to your son. What do you think you were doing when you running around town cheating all up and down on me?"

"I wasn't bringing any of those tricks around our son and no matter what I took care of home because my son has always been number one. "

"So you don't think that hurting me the way you did affected your son? You must be out of your mind if you think I'm just supposed to put my life on hold because you are CJ's father. I want to move on and be happy in a real relationship with a faithful man!"

"You don't really even know this guy to know if he's faithful or not."

"Well I think it's worth taking the chance to find out. I can't do this anymore Corey."

Corey's anger showed all over his face. It was like he went from Dr. Jekyll to Mr. Hyde. He snatched the flowers out of her hand and threw them against the wall. "Fuck you Unique and Fuck that dude. I can't believe you would play me like this! After all I've been going through with you over the last year."

"After all that you've been going through. Please spare me the BS." They stared each other down for a few seconds. She stormed over and opened the front door. "Get the fuck out!"

Corey was mean-mugging her. "You better be glad I don't hit women."

He punched a hole in her wall and left slamming her storm door so hard that the glass fell out and broke.

****

Shauntel and Nate were on their way to the club so that Shauntel could supervise the party planner's finishing touches on the decorations. She knew that she needed to have an uncomfortable conversation with Nate and it was time to stop avoiding it and talk to him about it now. She reached over and rubbed his thigh. He was instantly aroused. There was something about her touch that he never experienced with any other woman. "Girl you'd better stop before I have to pull over and snatch you in the back seat."

She giggled and playfully punched his arm. "You are so nasty."

He quickly retorted. "But you like it though."

She looked at him. "Nate do you remember the guy Mike I told you about before?"

"Yeah. What about him?"

"I want you to meet him."

"Why would I want to do that?"

She was hesitant in her explanation. "It's just that he is the only guy beside you who has ever truly been there for me. I know it may sound crazy but I look up to him like a father figure and after thinking about it for a very long time, he is the only person I could think of that really has earned a right to give me away to you at our wedding."

Nate looked at her like she was crazy. "Tel you have to be kidding. You want me to sign off on a guy you used to get down with giving you away at our wedding?"

She tried to reassure him. "It's not like that with me and him. He is more like family than any other man I can think about. You would really like Mike and he wants us to be happy."

Nate was gazing at her in amazement just a little too long. "Nate watch out for that car!" When Nate looked up he was too close to the car in front of him to stop in time. He had to swerve the SUV to the right and slam on his brakes to avoid a collision. He drove into a ditch and had to call his roadside assistance to come and get them towed out. While they waited for the tow service, their conversation got really heated. Nate really didn't want to talk about it, but Shauntel was not letting up because the wedding was right around the corner and she needed to tie up all of the loose ends. She had gone over it in her mind millions of times and could not even consider anyone else to give her away.

"Look Nate, me and Mike have not been physically involved in so long that we don't even look at each other like that. " He is actually happy for us and wants us to have the best. You know that I always keep it real no matter how somebody might take it. I don't want him and he doesn't want me."

"I hear all of that, but I'm just not feeling that Tel. Why can't one of your cousins give you away?"

"Which one of my cousins have you ever even met?"

"None, but what does that mean?"

"That means that I don't talk to them like that. I want somebody who really cares about my happiness and well being to give me away. All I'm asking you to do is meet with him and then you can decide from there."

"I'm really not trying to hear that right now! I don't want to meet that dude. I might have to swing on him just on the principle that he used to get busy with you. Are you sure you want to put him in that kind of predicament?"

Shauntel was really growing impatient with him because she felt like he was really being immature. She folded her arms, huffed and puffed, and laid her seat back. "Whatever, Nate. Forget it!"

"I know you are not getting mad. How would you feel if the tables were reversed? What if I asked you to let one of my ex-girlfriends be one of your bridesmaids? Would you be down with that?"

If looks could kill he would have been dead right there in that ditch. But, she played it cool because she really wanted to sway him her way. "Yes I would be okay with it as long as you assured me that it was innocent. That's because I trust you though. Apparently you don't trust me."

He raised his voice. "Don't throw that trust excuse in there on me. I do trust you! And that's BS, you would not be having my ex up in your wedding party. I just feel like that shit is disrespectful."

Shauntel was fuming. She felt like he was making a whole lot of something out of nothing. She turned her head to look out of the window. "Nate I'm done talking about it." Her feelings were hurt because she was really looking forward to Mike walking her down the aisle. She did not talk to him anymore the whole time they waited for the tow truck or on the way to the club. He tried to apologize and strike up a conversation, but she was too mad that he yelled at her unnecessarily. She was going to make him suffer and eventually she would get her way.

****

Nate and Shauntel had never been in such an uncomfortable situation. They didn't want to let on to the people there that they were having a tense moment, so they had to pretend that everything was perfect for the next few hours. Shauntel walked in and apologized to the owner of the Party Planning Company for being late. They were already halfway done with all of the decorations. She had requested a few changes at the last meeting and the planner was just there waiting for Shauntel to come and give her approval on the changes. Nate tried to make himself look busy so that he would not have to have any direct conversation with Shauntel in front strangers. He didn't want her to start screaming at him while they were there. It took about three hours for her to give her approval and for the workers to get everything set up just perfectly. Shauntel walked out of the door and walked back in so that she can get the full effect of what people would see the next night when they walked in. She walked through one last time and was thoroughly pleased. So she paid the party planner and went to wait in the car while Nate locked up the club. She sent Tasha a text message to let her know that everything was a go and that she would be pleased.

When Nate came back to the car, he was still trying to strike up a conversation with her. However, she was still pissed off and kept her responses as short as possible if she even responded at all. Finally, he got the point and decided to give her time to cool off. When he pulled up to the house, she barely gave him a chance to stop before she was opening her door and storming to her car.

He yelled behind her. "Shauntel!"

She didn't even turn around. She got in her car, started the engine and peeled out. He just stood in the yard shaking his head in disgust. Shauntel had a hair and nail appointment so she blasted her Mary J. Blige

CD, hopped on the freeway and headed to the beauty salon. She was in the need for some pampering and she decided to get the works. She got her hair done, her nails done, a pedicure, an eyebrow wax and a set of extra long individual lashes. She never wore false lashes but she felt like doing something different so she went with the flow. When she looked in the mirror she was amazed at the transformation. She knew the false lashes were going to take some time to get used to but they were tastefully beautiful because of her big almond shaped eyes. All of the customers in the shop were raving about how beautiful she looked and how Nate better watch his back or else she might get snatched. Shauntel hung around for a few minutes chatting the normal beauty shop gossip. Then she decided that she was going to indulge in some retail therapy to relieve some stress. She headed to the mall and had a mini shopping spree and an hour full body massage.

CHAPTER 11

*T*asha was so excited about her birthday party. She and Shauntel had put every effort they had into making sure it was going to be remembered as the event of the year. She was putting the finishing touches on her makeup and looking in the mirror at what she considered perfection. She was wearing a black fitted Versace dress with a plunging neckline. The girls were sitting up perfectly thanks to the double-sided tape she had applied. Her dress was long and snatched at the waist with a split all the way up the thigh that stopped just below her sweet spot. She had adorned her dress with pure red diamond accessories to match her red bottom stilettos. She'd had her hair spiral curled and swept up into an up-do with a few curls dangling down. She finished up by putting on her red Mac lipstick. She was set and ready to go when her doorbell rang. She grabbed her red clutch and headed for the door. She opened the door to see what appeared to be a very old man standing there in a tuxedo and Shauntel getting out of the back of the Jaguar Limousine. The limousine driver was grey all over and looked as if he had lost some inches in height over the years. However, you could still see that he had been very handsome in his day. "Good evening Ms. Thornton. Are you ready?"

"As ready as I'll ever be."

He offered her his arm to usher her to the car. She put her arm in his and started down the steps when she noticed Shauntel outside of the car looking like a movie star in her black satin ball gown adorned with silver beads across the top and sheer beaded cap sleeves. Her hair was elegantly pulled up into a bun and she wore diamond dangling earrings and silver studded stilettos. They both got excited when they saw each other and did the *girl scream*. "They followed up the screams with "you look so pretty," "no you look so pretty," we are going to be killing 'em tonight." After taking some magazine appropriate pictures, they got back in the limo and headed to the club to have the time of their lives.

The limo pulled up to the front door of the club and Tasha and Shauntel had their last toast and downed their glasses of Champagne before stepping out of the Limo and heading to the red carpet. It actually looked like a real red carpet event. The carpet was sprinkled with gold rose petals. There were cameras everywhere as people posed on the red carpet. The celebrity light shone so bright that the surrounding area looked pitch black. Shauntel had even arranged for a local lady radio emcee to interview the guests and ask them what they were wearing like on the real red carpet. Tasha and Shauntel took a couple of pictures together on the red carpet and then Tasha all but did her own private photo shoot with the photographers. After her photo shoot, the girls made their way into the club. Tasha was floored at how beautiful the club looked and it showed on her face. The theme was thirty and flirty. There was a huge wall with a mural of the number 30 on it that displayed 30 pictures of Tasha over her lifetime. Under the thirty were the words "And Flirty". There was a huge chandelier in the middle of the ceiling with white sheer fabric swooping down from it adorned in white lights. The tables had gold tablecloths on them that looked like miniskirts with two oversized crystal candleholders that burned gold shimmery candles at each end of the table. Each candleholder bottom was wrapped in two dozens of red roses. There were gold sparkling champagne glasses all over the table and a complimentary bottle of Krug, Clos du Mesnil 1995 Champagne. There were red placemats with gold plates and gold utensils placed perfectly on top. The chairs were covered in satin gold cloth with red bows tied around them. Tasha turned to Shauntel.

"This is more than I expected. Thank you so much. Girl, you are the bomb!" She hugged Shauntel tight.

"Girl you don't have to thank me. We are family and you know I had to make it hot for my only sister. Now let's get our party on."

Nate had gotten to the club early to make sure that his security was ready and everyone knew what their jobs were. Nate did not want to be too dressy because even though he had taken the night off, he still had to watch his staff's back in case anything jumped off. He wore some dark true religion jeans with a black and silver striped button up, silk sliver tie and a black blazer. He finished it off with black Ralph Lauren boots and an oyster white gold Rolex. He was looking like he stepped fresh out of GQ. He knew that Shauntel was still mad at him but she had put aside their differences for now so that they could enjoy the evening. As soon as she laid her eyes on him she bit down on her lip. He was looking so sexy that she wanted to jump his bones right then and there. After Shauntel got settled, he took her out on the red carpet so that they could take some pictures together. They took a few nice pictures and then he took her out on the dance floor and ballroom danced with her. Most people wouldn't think that Nate could dance because of his size. But working security in the club had really paid off in regard to his dancing skills. They set the club off with a fancy ballroom routine. At the end of the dance he pulled her into him and looked her in the eye. "I'm sorry Tel." Then he tongued her down. She was tingling all over. He made it so hard for her to be mad at him. She surrendered to his kiss and released the anger. But the conversation still wasn't over for her. Mike was going to give her away and that was that!

The night was amazing. There were local celebrities on the rise there to perform including a new rapper from Grand Rapids and an R&B duo who made you feel like you were watching Rick James and Teena Marie. In between performances the DJ was playing all of the hottest hits and Shauntel and Tasha didn't waste any time dropping it like it was hot on the dance floor! In the middle of the night, Nate brought Corey over to the table and introduced him to Tasha.

"Tasha this is my boy Corey. Corey this is Tasha." Corey extended his hand and made sure he got a firm grip on her hand before he covered the backside of her hand with his other hand.

"Happy Birthday Ma."

She was wondering if he was flirting with her, but she wasn't sure. She was already a little tipsy from all of the champagne she had been drinking. "Thank you. Would you like some champagne?"

"No thanks. I don't drink while I'm on the job. I do dance though, so why don't you save me a birthday dance?"

Tasha wasn't normally friendly with new guys but something about him made her feel comfortable. Plus, the alcohol had allowed her to let her wall down. "I guess I could do that."

"That's what's up. Remember that if you have any problems or need anything, Corey is your man." He tapped his muscular chest, which drew her attention to his huge pecks. She thought '*damn he must live in the gym*'. It had been a minute since she had any loving and he was making her moist so she snapped herself back to her senses and forced herself to stop smiling so wide. "Okay Corey I will keep that in mind." He finally let go of her hand.

The party continued with a few more performances and it was time to sing Happy Birthday. There was an R&B quartet group that led the crowd in singing Happy Birthday in harmony. It was off the chain. After Tasha blew out the candles, it was time to take the 30 balloons with the 30 wishes in them and let them loose. As the balloons ascended into the sky, Tasha got emotional and started crying. She was crying happy tears for the first time in a long time. "Shauntel you made this night so special. Thank you so much."

"Girl it's nothing. You deserve it."

They hugged each other and Tasha was squeezing like her life depended on it. They went back inside and had a few birthday toasts. By the time the toast was over Tasha had drank another two glasses of champagne, downing one of them. Just then Corey came over and tapped her on the shoulder.

"Did you save that dance for me Ms. Tasha?"

She smiled wide again. "It must be your lucky day, because I sure did."

He led her out on the dance floor and they danced to at least 6 songs non-stop. Tasha leaned into his ear. "I'm burning up. I'm going to have to take a break. Maybe we can pick up where we left off later."

Corey leaned in really close making sure his lips touched her ear. "I could dance with you all night. But I understand. We *will* pick it up later." As Tasha made her way back to the table Nate was going to check on things to make sure everything was secure. Her words were loud. "I'm burning up and thirsty." She grabbed her glassed and filled it with champagne and downed it. A few minutes later the champagne hit her when she tried to stand up to go to the bathroom. She stumbled. Shauntel looked at her strange.

"Are you okay Tasha?"

"I'm okay. I think I shouldn't have taken that last drink. I just need a minute."

"Well just sit down for a minute I'll go get you some water." Shauntel looked up and Byron was staring right in her face. She couldn't believe her eyes. She was staring at a dead man.

"So you thought it was going to be that easy to play me to the left Shauntel?"

She was caught off guard and confused as to why he was even talking to her. "Byron what are you talking about?"

"You know damn well what I'm talking about. I know that you're pregnant with my baby and you're trying to have that softy you call a man be a stand in daddy to my baby."

She couldn't believe what she was hearing. "I don't know what crazy bus you just got off of but I am *not* pregnant with your baby!"

"Bitch don't lie to me. You are not going to keep my baby from me."

She was irritated at the nerve of him.

"Look Byron, trust me when I tell you that you don't want to do this here. Now my advice to you is to back the fuck up out of my face and make a swift exit or you're gonna be sorry!" She started to walk off. He snatched her back by her arm. "You're the one whose gonna be sorry if you think for one minute I'm not going to be a part of my child's life. So you can tell ole boy to bounce." His grip was tight on her and she knew this could go very wrong very fast and she didn't want to ruin Tasha's party. So she tried to snatch her arm away from him with at least force as possible. "Byron let me go!"

He tightened his grip. "Bitch I'm not playing with you!"

Tasha was trying to grasp what was going on but things were a little blurry. She thought she saw Byron snatching Shauntel up but she wasn't sure. At that moment she became angry with herself for allowing herself to get drunk and in a state that she couldn't help Shauntel out. All of a sudden Nate socked Byron dead in his jaw and he went sliding across the floor. He had spotted Byron grabbing her from across the room.

"Tel who the fuck is that clown?"

"Baby that's Byron."

Nate looked like he had seen a ghost. Byron was trying his best to get up off of the floor but as soon as he was able to stagger to his feet, Nate rushed him slamming back to the floor hard. The fall coupled with the weight of Nate's body falling on top of him, knocked all of the wind from his lungs. He was gasping for air as Nate stood up and commenced to stumping him everywhere that he could. Corey and another bouncer rushed over and drug Nate off of him. "Chill out Nate. You're going to kill him."

Nate snatched away from them. "Get off me!"

He walked over to Shauntel to make sure she was okay. Corey and the other bouncer snatched Byron off the floor and drug him toward the door. He was yelling out obscenities. "Bitch you know that's my baby. I'm going to see my baby."

The crowd that had formed started to disperse. People started walking over to Tasha giving her hugs and telling her bye. She was so drunk that she could hardly make out who was who. Shauntel went to get Tasha two glasses of ice water and she was trying to drink them as fast as possible.

Byron was still outside being rowdy, yelling and screaming obscenities. Corey was fed up with this idiot. He mean-mugged Byron. "Look bro if you don't get the fuck out of here, that ass whooping you just took from my homeboy is not even going to compare to what I'm getting ready to do to you! That's your final warning!"

Things happened so fast. Byron pulled out a gun and started shooting wildly. People were screaming, hollering, running and pushing frantically. In the midst of all the commotion, Corey was pushed to the ground and was unable to get to his gun fast enough. It took Corey a second to get up from the ground. By the time he did, the shooting had stopped and he was not able to spot Byron anywhere. There were sounds of people burning rubber while trying to get away from the danger. Inside the club, Shauntel had to push Tasha to the ground because she was just sitting up as if gunshots were not being fired. Nate was able to make his way outside quickly but the incident was over so fast that by the time he made it, the crowd was too much for him to even try to find Byron. He was able to get to Corey though and see that he was okay and hadn't been shot. They made their way back into the club to make sure that the girls were alright. So far it looked like nobody had been harmed. But both of the girls were pretty shook up. Nate helped them both off of the floor. Then the police sirens sounded like about 100 cars were coming. Corey filled Nate in on what had happened before the police came in with all of their questions. They came to an agreement that they would stick to the hood code of not saying anything. *'Snitches get stitches.'* They stayed until the police were finished with all of their questions. By that time, it was 2:30 in the morning. Nate and Corey decided that they would handle Byron later on because they had to get some info on him first.

Tasha was feeling much better after all of the water she drank and her many trips to the restroom, but she was still pretty tipsy. Her limo driver had left the club during all of the chaos. Nate asked Corey to take her home and he agreed. They left the club after Shauntel gave Corey strict instructions. "Before you go anywhere, stop at the gas station and get her a bottle of water so that she can sober up."

They all said their goodbyes and Corey did as he was told. He stopped at the nearest gas station and got Tasha a bottle of water and a pain pill so that she wouldn't have a hangover the next day. He got back in the truck and she was kind of slouched down in the seat with her eyes closed. He gently nudged her. "Are you alright?"

She sat up straight. "I'm fine. I just need some air."

He cracked her window, gave her the water and pain pill and started on his way to her house following her directions.

They made small talk on the way and made it to her house in about 15 minutes.

"Thanks for bringing me home Corey."

"Don't mention it. Let me carry you in the house so that you don't fall and hurt yourself."

"I don't need you to carry me. I'm fine."

He gave her a skeptical look. "Are you sure?"

"Yes. If you don't believe me, you can walk me in to make sure."

He walked her into the house. Once he was inside, he noticed how attracted he really was to Tasha. Even in her drunken state, she was sexy to him. Her full lips were turning him on. He figured he would strike up a conversation so that his head below wouldn't take control. "Yo, your place is nice!"

"Thanks. I do interior decorating and party planning for a living so I can't have my place looking wrong. You hungry or want something to drink?"

"What do you have bartender?"

She giggled. "I've got whatever you need. What is your drink of choice?"

"Do you have Whiskey?"

"*Whiskey?* Who drinks Whiskey in the 21st century?"

"I do. Now do you have some?"

"I told you I have whatever you need. Would you like that on the rocks?"

"No. Straight up bartender."

She went into the kitchen and poured him a double shot of Jack Daniels. He got comfortable on her oversized sectional while he waited. As soon as she handed it to him, he downed it with no hesitation.

"I'll fix you another one." She made her way back to the kitchen and refilled his drink. She came back and handed it to him. He sipped it this time.

"I have to go take these clothes off and get comfortable. Make yourself at home. I'll be right back."

Corey did as he was told and turned on the TV to ESPN while sipping on his whiskey. A few minutes later Tasha came down the stairs wearing jeggings and a tank top. She sat down next to him. He was in deep thought. *'Damn this chick is sexy as hell and she seems like she has a good head on her shoulders.'*

"Thank you for making sure I had what I needed to come down from that alcohol."

"You're welcome."

"I wanted my party to be the party of the year to remember, but not in that way. That clown was foolin'."

"Yeah, he was. He'd better be glad that I wasn't able to get to my heat in time to lay him out."

"He is crazy."

"He ain't seen crazy, but trust me he will."

Tasha didn't want to know any details so she changed the subject. "So tell me about Corey."

"There isn't much to tell. I'm a down to earth guy who minds his own business. I have one son who is my heart. Me and his mother have a messed up relationship because I messed up so many times with her. When she got pregnant, I wasn't really ready to settle down. I cheated on her over and over again and I regret that because she was the kind of chick you could take home to mother. She is not willing to let that go so I have to move on. I have been doing security work most of my life and I love it. I want to eventually own my own business, but I have been trying to help Nate get his situated first. Other than that, I'm just a man looking for the right woman to complete me. Now that I'm a *grown ass* man, I'm ready to settle down. What about you?"

"I am a lot more complicated than that. I won't burden you with all of my drama. But, I will just say that I am trying to bounce back from some horrible situations. In the meantime, I throw myself into my work so that I don't have to worry so much about my past. I have never really had a real relationship and I have no kids or family."

He moved closer to her. "Ms. Tasha, it sounds like you could really use a friend."

She smelled his Versace cologne and like it a lot. "I guess I really could."

He moved even closer. "So could I."

He grabbed the back off her head and kissed her intensely. She kissed him back and from there it was on and popping!

****

Shauntel woke up the next day feeling really good. She had really put it on Nate the night before. She knew that he was completely stressed out with the Byron situation. As soon as they got home, she ran him a hot bath and let him soak for a few minutes. She put on some sexy lingerie and went into the bathroom and washed him up really well. Then she took him to bed and gave him some satisfying oral pleasure before riding him until he was convulsing. Needless to say, the next morning he had agreed to meet with Mike and consider letting him give her away at their wedding.

Shauntel didn't really do much the day after the party. She used that day to recuperate so that she would be ready for court the next day. Nate had left the house for a couple of hours to handle some business. While he was out, she called Mike so that she could set up the meeting between him and Nate. She told him that she needed to see him and have an important conversation with him. He agreed to meet her the next day after her court hearing. When Nate got back she told him that she was going to meet with Mike and tell him what she wanted so that they could meet and discuss him giving her away. They watched basketball games all day and went to bed early so that they could both be up early for court.

****

Tasha woke up Sunday afternoon feeling just a little off. It was 1:00. It took a minute for her to realize that she was in her bed. She looked over and saw Corey lying next to her and that is when the events of the night before started to flood her memory. She remembered the fight between Nate and Byron and how Byron had started shooting completely ruining her party. Then she thought about the limo driver leaving her at the club and she was mad. The more she thought about it though, she really couldn't be mad at him. After all, he was an elderly man in the midst of gunshots. The smart thing to do was to leave. So she put aside her initial thoughts of calling the limousine company and complaining. Then she remembered how caring Corey had seemed and how his passionate kiss had led into them making love almost all night long. After he had kissed her, he seductively started to undress her, sucking and licking every inch of her body from her face to her toes. He had made her climax so many times with his head between her legs that she couldn't even count. Then he carried her up to her bedroom and continued to please her sexually with his thick manhood for the next few hours. Remembering the events of the night before made her realize the pleasant soreness between her legs. Corey started to stir. She looked over at his chiseled body. "Good morning sleepy head."

"Good morning sexy. You sure know how to wear a brother out."

"I'm the one who's worn out from that thick stick you were working in and out of me."

He pulled the cover off of him displaying his huge erection. "And he's ready to go to work again. Why don't you come and sit on him?"

She hopped up on top of him. He wet his fingers and massaged her clit. He stuck two fingers inside of her and used his thumb to continue to massage her clit while working his fingers in and out of her. She grinded against his hand and was dripping wet in minutes. He reached over on the nightstand and grabbed a condom. He slipped it on and entered her slowly. She was riding him like she was in a rodeo. He admired her pretty perfect breasts and wondered if they were real. There wasn't one flaw on either of them. Her big round nipples made him want to taste them. He pulled her breasts into his face and admired them up close before devouring them with his mouth. She screamed his name out in ecstasy and that sent him through the roof. He tried to pound her as deep as her insides would allow. They had sex for the next few hours making each other climax over and over again. When they were finally done, they took a shower together. They had a water fight in the shower. Tasha started it by cupping her hands under the shower water and letting them fill up before throwing the water in Corey's face. "Oh you want to play water fight with the reigning champ?"

Tasha put her hands on her naked hips. "Reigning champ? That was before you met me, the super soaker."

He reached out of the shower and grabbed the decorative cup that was on the sink. "I can show you better than I can tell you."

Before she could even try to protect herself, he had filled the cup up with water and drenched her. She stood under the water and closed her eyes slapping the water in Corey's direction. In his attempt to duck the water, he dropped the cup. Tasha opened her eyes to the sound of the cup crashing to the tub floor. She bent down quickly and grabbed the cup and filled it up. As she tried to throw it on him, he grabbed her and pulled her so close to him that if she would have thrown the water on him it would have landed on her too. He passionately engulfed her lips with her mouth and she kissed him back. He spent her around so that she was facing the wall. He licked the back of her neck and whispered in her ear. "Let me see how wet the super soaker is." He inserted his finger inside her hole from behind and nibbled on her ear. She put both of her hands up on the shower wall and bucked back on his fingers. She moaned loudly as her clit quickly swelled. He took his fingers out and smoothly replaced them with his massive erection. He reached his hand around to the front of her body and massaged her clit while he rhythmically filled her up from the back until they both climaxed together. They washed each other's bodies while they tried to bring their breathing back to normal. After they got dressed, Corey took her out to eat at local Italian restaurant. They decided to go back to his place after dinner.

****

Corey's house was nicely built. It was obvious that it was a new structure. It was a 5-bedroom colonial. Everything looked sparkling new including the Italian carpet, stainless steel appliances and the hardwood floors that led from the lowered entrance through the French doors into the huge dining room. The only thing the house was missing was the appropriate furniture and decoration.

"I haven't been here long enough to really furnish it," he told her as he gave her a tour of the house.

"Corey, this is beautiful."

"I'm glad you like it. Maybe you can help me with the decorating Ms. Interior Decorator.

She smiled at him. "I'm not sure that you can afford me."

"Maybe I could pay you in another way." He wrapped his arms around her cupping her butt with both of his hands. He pulled her into him. She allowed him to pull her closer.

"And how would that be?"

"I can show you better than I can tell you." Why don't you spend the night?"

Before she could answer, he kissed her passionately. When they broke their kiss, they stared into each other's eyes.

She broke the silence. "I guess I could consider that."

He walked her upstairs and showed her the other three bedrooms, the half bath and the master bathroom. The master bathroom was like another house. It had a stand-alone shower and his and her sinks. The master bedroom had two huge walk-in closets and was the only room with a bed. The bed was round and covered in earth tone linens.

"Corey, why do you need all of this house?"

"I really don't. I got it at a steal though. The previous owners lost the house because of unpaid property taxes. I was just going to stay here until I found another place and then sale it for a lot more than I paid for it. Unless I meet the woman of my dreams and she wants to give me a whole bunch of babies to fill up all of these empty rooms."

"What? I'm not the woman of your dreams?"

He cocked his head to the side. "I'm not sure. Maybe I'd be able to better decide if you would practice with me on making that bunch of babies."

"Oh really?' She untied the straps on her wrap dress. She pulled the dress off letting it hit the floor exposing her black lace Victoria Secret bra and thong. She pushed him down on the bed and mounted him.

****

Tasha woke up in the middle of the night and Corey wasn't next to her. She noticed it was cold in the house. She reached over on the nightstand and grabbed her cell phone. She pushed the power button illuminating the screen. The time read 3:33 AM. She sat up in the bed and looked around using the cell phone light. She decided to go look for Corey. She continued to use the cell phone light to walk through the house so that she wouldn't bump into anything. She didn't know where any of the light switches were. After a quick sweep of the upstairs, she went downstairs and noticed a light coming from the kitchen. She walked in and peeked around the corner.

He was at the kitchen sink filling a small glass with water from the faucet.

"I thought you left me."

Startled, Corey dropped the bottle of prescription pills that he had just picked up. The pills fell all over the kitchen floor.

"Girl you'd better learn how to make some noise."

"I'm sorry but I was cold. Can you turn on the heat?"

He walked over to her and scooped her up in his arms. "I've got something better than heat to warm you up!"

"Don't you need to take your medicine?"

"They're just muscle relaxers for my back strain. I hate taking pills anyway. Besides, your medicine works much better than those pills." He carried her back to bed and did exactly what he had promised, warmed her up.

CHAPTER 12

*T*he stylist arrived at the house bright and early. She was ringing the doorbell at 7:00 AM. Shauntel was glad that she hadn't been able to sleep because of her nerves. She had already showered and ate breakfast. They had met the week before for a final fitting of the navy blue suit they agreed on after it had been tailored. The jacket was trimmed in white at the collar and around the pockets with three white buttons down the front. She wore a navy blue pleated hem skirt with thin white trim around the bottom of the skirt. The stylist picked out a simple pair of genuine pearl earrings and navy blue pumps. She flat ironed Shauntel's hair and pulled it back into a ponytail. They chose flesh toned panty hose. She put on a light coat of makeup, just a bit of eye shadow and a very light lip-gloss. When she was finished Shauntel looked in the mirror and was surprisingly satisfied. She looked conservative, but stylish. The stylist was the bomb! She did all of that in about 30 minutes and they were ready to go so that they could meet with the attorney at 8:00 before her hearing began at 9:00.

Shauntel and Nate arrived at the courthouse right at 8:00 AM. They had not prepared for standing in the ridiculously long line to go through the metal detector before actually making it into the court. Shauntel had never been to court before so this was all new to her. She was shocked at how many people were being sent back to their cars because of the things they had in their pockets and purses. She would have been pissed off if she would have had to leave and come back and stand in that long line. Luckily, she had actually read the court papers that told you everything that was not allowed in the court. They finally made it to the hallway of the courtroom where her case was scheduled about 15 minutes later. The attorney's assistant ushered them into a small conference room that was reserved for attorneys and their clients. A few minutes later Attorney Hartford entered the room shaking both of their hands before taking his seat.

"Shauntel, how are you feeling?"

Her anxiety showed in her face. "Nervous as hell."

He reassured her. "Don't be. You're in good hands now. I have gone over both Mr. Whittington's and Ms. Thornton's statements and they will be very helpful. Also, I told you that this case is all circumstantial.

Circumstantial evidence doesn't win cases when you have a smart defense attorney. Let me remind you that there is a very good chance that the judge will find that there is enough probable cause to proceed to trial. The evidence that is presented today doesn't have to be solid. The prosecution just basically needs to convince the judge that there is a chance that you may have committed the crimes you are charged with. Rest assured that I am going to do everything possible to end this today though. I just want to be realistic with you that it may not end today. If it doesn't though, the prosecution doesn't stand a chance against us at trial. Their evidence does not prove you guilty beyond a reasonable doubt. That is their burden all we have to do is make sure that the jury is aware of that reasonable doubt if this does go to trial. I am confident that we will win this."

He patted her on the back. "Relax."

She exhaled and shook her head in agreement. "Okay."

"Do either of you have any questions?"

They said in unison. "No."

"Ok let me know if you do before the hearing starts." Attorney Hartford left the room and Nate grabbed her and held her tight. "Tel, I'm here for you through it all and everything is going to be okay." He massaged her back to help her relax.

Shauntel whispered. "What if he's wrong?"

****

The hearing did not start until after 11:00. Shauntel was so anxious by then that she had sweated her hair out and it had curled up. So now she had a curly ponytail. Thank goodness that it still looked professional. The prosecution's first witness was officer Durham, the pudgy white cop who had come to the hospital with all of the incriminating questions. He looked like he had his head stuck up his butt. Even though Shauntel was disgusted with him, she took her Attorney's advice and kept a neutral serious face. The prosecutor was a tall slender young white man who looked like he had never had fun in his life. He went through all of the irrelevant questions.

"State your name for the record please."

"What is your position for the Detroit Police Department?"

"How long have you been a Detroit Police Officer?"

Finally, he got to the stuff that actually mattered. "On the date of January twenty-seventh two thousand and sixteen, were you called to investigate a possible arson?"

"Yes I was."

"Did you have a discussion with fire department investigators when you arrived?"

"Yes. When my partner and I first arrived we talked to the investigators, they informed us that their initial assessment was that the fire had been intentionally set."

"How did they arrive at that determination?"

"They inspected the whole house and found that there was only one hot spot in the entire home. That hot spot was the middle of the living room and looked like a huge pile of clothes had been set on fire in that spot. There was also evidence that an accelerant had been used. There was no evidence of anything that could have caused the fire without intent."

"What was the next step in the investigation?"

"Determining how the arsonist had entered the property."

"Were you able to determine that?"

"We were able to determine that there had been no forced entry into the home. So whoever set the fire was either let into the home or had a key."

"Is that why you questioned the owner of the property, Shauntel Barnes?"

"Yes. My partner and I went right over to the hospital to get a statement from Ms. Barnes in an attempt to get some clarification of what may have happened."

Shauntel was cringing in her seat because they were making her sound so guilty.

The prosecutor continued. "Was Ms. Barnes cooperative?"

"Not really. She and her boyfriend were quite confrontational."

"Did Ms. Barnes at least give you logical explanation of how this may have happened?"

"No she just claimed to be at her boyfriend's house at the time of the fire and said she had not left anyone in her home."

"What do you believe happened on the day of January twenty-seventh Officer Durham?"

"I believe that Shauntel Barnes set her own home on fire so that she could take advantage of her hefty home owner's insurance claim."

"And how much would that claim be worth?"

"A million dollars."

There were loud gasps in the courtroom and some people just shifted in their seats.

"No further questions your Honor." The prosecutor dramatically returned to his seat.

Attorney Hartford approached the witness stand. "Good afternoon Officer Durham."

Officer Durham's aggravation with the defense attorney showed already. "Good Afternoon."

"You said that my client and her *fiancé* were confrontational. Would you mind explaining exactly what you mean by that?"

"Well her boyfriend..."

Attorney Hartford interrupted. "Fiancé."

The officer was a little flustered. "Yeah. Her fiancé basically interrupted our questions before we were allowed to really get any information."

"Were you aware that Ms. Barnes and her fiancé had just been made aware that she was pregnant literally seconds before you entered the room to interrogate them?"

He had caught the officer off guard again. "No and it wasn't an interrogation."

"What would you call it Officer Durham?"

"I would call it a questioning."

"A questioning huh? When you went to the hospital to *question* Ms. Barnes, hadn't she just been rushed to the hospital because she lost consciousness from the surprise of witnessing her home on fire? And don't you think seeing your house burn to the ground and being surprisingly told that you're pregnant within just a few minutes would make a woman a little impatient?"

"I wouldn't know."

"Officer Durham it sounds like you did not cover too many bases in regard to the circumstances surrounding this case. Did you or your partner consider any other leads before arresting my client?"

"No. The evidence...."

Attorney Hartford cut him off again. "Have you *ever* considered any other possible leads?"

"There were not any other leads."

"Or did you just not even consider that there could be? No further questions for this witness."

Shauntel felt a little redeemed as her lawyer took his seat next to her at the defense table. The prosecution called Officer Durham's partner Officer Thornton to the stand and asked her almost identical questions to the ones he had asked Officer Durham. She accomplished the same task of making Shauntel sound guilty. Shauntel's attorney followed with the same intense cross-examination putting wholes in Officer Thornton's seemingly airtight testimony.

The judge followed with, "Let me preface my decision by saying that this case is significant in that it is right on the borderline of satisfying probable cause. However, I find that there is enough probable cause to take this case to trial. A word of caution to the prosecution, I would suggest that you bring more evidence to trial than what you have here today. What you have is circumstantial at best. Trial is set for May seventh two thousand and sixteen."

With that, the judge banged her gavel. Attorney Hartford ushered Shauntel and Nate out of the courtroom and back into the conference room.

Shauntel's nervousness had returned and was written all over her face. "What does this mean?"

Attorney Hartford gestured for them to take a seat. "You heard the advice the judge gave the prosecution. She noticed the same thing I mentioned to you earlier. As long as you didn't do this, you have nothing to worry about. I don't see a way of them coming to trial with more evidence than they had today. There is no physical evidence or witnesses to say that you did this. Without any of those things, I don't see a jury finding you guilty beyond a reasonable doubt."

Shauntel took a deep breath. "This is nerve wrecking."

Nate reached over and rubbed her lower back.

Attorney Hartford wanted to calm their fears. "I don't want you two to let this consume you. Please try your best to relax until after the trial. I will be in touch in a few weeks so that we can schedule a date for the stylist to come back to help with your wardrobe for trial."

CHAPTER 13

.....A month later

*T*he wedding was incomparable to anything either Shauntel or Nate had ever even imagined. The colors were purple with a hint of baby blue so that they both were able to enjoy their favorite colors. The venue was the Iced Hotel in one of the oversized banquet rooms and the decorations were absolutely exquisite. There was a huge crystal Chandelier in the middle of the room with a few blue and purple light bulbs sprinkled throughout. The cathedral ceiling was covered with a lighted sheer cloth with hints of blue cascading down on the room. There was a white 5 tier cake set up on the cake table adorned with purple trim, silver pearls and a blue bouquet of flowers on top and at the bottom left side. The tables were adorned with dark purple tablecloths, baby blue flowers spread around and huge silver candleholders with purple candles burning inside of them. The centerpieces were tall metal decorations in the shape of a tree with dozens of lit candles sitting on each branch. The many floor to ceiling windows were covered with shimmering white sheer drapes that picked up the light blue and purple iridescent shadows from the light of the many candles burning. There was an assortment of wine glasses and champagne flutes spread around the table in different shapes and sizes. There was a silver china and silverware setting at every seat. The ceremony started with Shauntel's cousin, Erica singing a remixed rendition of Stevie Wonder's *"Ribbon In The Sky"*. There wasn't a dry eye in the place when she was done. The wedding party was serenaded into the room to an instrumental of "Ribbon In The Sky" that the organist played. Nate and the Minister were standing at the far end of the room under a well-lit decorated arch. Erica walked down the aisle first in an iridescent off the shoulder dress. Harmony followed her in an identical dress in a larger size. Next Corey walked Tasha down the aisle arm in arm. She wore a long lavender one-shoulder fitted dress with an asymmetrical skirt. It was covered with sheer and there was one baby blue flower on the top right. All of the bridesmaids wore a variety of curly pinned up hairstyles. Corey walked Tasha down to the front of the bridesmaid line, walked around her then kneeled down on one knee. He kissed her hand and gave her one long stemmed purple rose. Corey's little cousin who was three years old walked in as the ring bearer holding the ring bearer's pillow. He had so much charisma that he stole the whole crowd's hearts. Harmony's five-year old daughter was up next in her beautiful organza dress with a ruffled skirt. She was carrying a flower basket adorned with purple and blue stones and filled with blue and purple flowers. She waited patiently for the bride's carpet to be laid out. She marched down to the arch dropping flower petals and waving to the crowd simultaneously. The double doors into the room were dramatically opened and the organist began his prelude to *"Here Comes The Bride"*. Shauntel stood just outside the doors with Mike on her arm. Nate had previously met with him and was pleasantly surprised that Mike was a cool guy. They had clicked immediately and Nate was proud to have him walk his bride down the aisle. Her dress was a strapless pick-up ball gown embellished with lace and shimmering stones. Her train looked as if it went for miles. Mike looked stylish as usual in an all white suit trimmed in purple with purple accessories. The crowd stood for the bride. Mike looked at her and smiled. "You ready?"

She took a deep breath. "I'm ready."

He walked her to the arch and gave her away to Nate with the preacher's leading. They had prepared their own vows. Shauntel went first:

"When I look at you, I see the other half of me. Until I met you I never imagined love could be absolutely perfect. Us two flawed people together make one perfect person. I submit my all to you and know that I will love you for eternity, through thick and thin, good and bad, ups and downs no matter what curves life throws us. Nathaniel Whittington, I am eternally yours until there is no longer breath in my body."

Nate was tearing up but he had to make it through his vows:

"Shauntel Barnes when God made you, he had me in mind. He couldn't have made a more perfect gift. Life without you equals death! I love you with every cord of my being. You are my sunshine. You are the reason I smile and the power that makes my heartbeat. I will forever love you and only you. I promise to protect you at all times and not just your safety but also everything that is dear to you. Before I met you, life was a blur. Now everything is so clear

and I look forward to making unimaginable memories with you as Mrs. Nathaniel Whittington. My whole life rest on making and keeping you happy until the day I die."

The ceremony was so heartfelt. Many grown men were crying. After the Minister pronounced them husband and wife, they took the most adoring photos and enjoyed the beginning of the celebration of their lives together. Shauntel wanted to go to Paris for their honeymoon. Instead they were on their way to Maui because the judge had made her surrender her passport.

****

Tasha and Corey had grown really close. They had been spending all of their free time together. She had even taken the time to decorate his entire house after he gave her his American Express card and told her to buy whatever she needed to make it feel like home. She really liked Corey but felt there was something strange about him that she just couldn't put her finger on. He could seem so close to her at times. Then at other times he was closed off and withdrawn. One morning a couple of weeks before the wedding after one of their hot sensual session, she woke up to an empty bed. She called him to find out why he had left without saying bye. He didn't answer his phone for three days. Then he just showed up at her house like nothing had ever happened. When she questioned him about it, he seemed nonchalant and changed the subject. Things were back to normal until the day after the wedding. She had a compelling suspicion that he was creeping back to his son's mother every now and then. She didn't like the idea, but really couldn't be upset because they had never agreed to be exclusive. She had to admit though; she had really strong feelings for Corey and was on the verge of falling in love with him.

She was in the kitchen cooking bacon, eggs, grits and cheese toast in her blue lace boy shorts and a tight white tank top humming the melody of Monica's *"Before You Walk Out My Life"* when Corey walked up behind her and wrapped his arms around her waist. He planted hot soft kisses on her neck and back. That made her temperature go through the roof.

"Hmmmm that smells good," he managed in between kisses.

"Hmmmm that feels good," She replied. "You'd better stop if you want to eat Mister."

He spun her around to face him and kissed her fervently.

"Corey, wait the food is going to burn!"

He reached behind her and turned the stove burners off. Then he picked her up and wrapped her legs around his waist. She felt his rock hard erection poke her in her wet spot. He sat her down on the kitchen island. "I'd rather eat you."

He knelt down in front of her and snatcher her legs open. He ripped her lace panties off and devoured her like it would be his last meal on earth. She leaned back and moaned while grinding against his hot wet lips and tongue over her clit rapidly. He inserted two fingers inside her hitting her g-spot while still licking and sucking on her sensitive spot. She started to jerk wildly. "Oh shit baby, I'm cumming." She exploded in his mouth. He sucked it all up not missing a drop. He stood up and kissed her making sure that she tasted her juices. He stretched her body out on the island and climbed on top of her giving her all 9.5 inches of him. He loved watching her huge breasts bounce as he pounded in and out of her.

"Take that shirt off so I can see those melons."

She took off her shirt and tossed it onto the floor. She was trying to match his pace but the sensation of all of that flesh going in and out of her rapidly was too much for her to bare. Within seconds she was climaxing again. He grabbed hold of her breasts never breaking his pace. She was dazed. He had never given it to her like this. His sex was always good, but this time it seemed like he anticipated her every need and he was satisfying her to no end. He pulled off his shirt and tossed it too. She admired his Adonis like physique. He was built like he lived in the gym. He continued his flow and once again her button was throbbing. He reached down and rubbed it in a circular motion while penetrating her even deeper. She was cumming again.

Once they were finished, Tasha had lost count of how many times she had climaxed. The room was spinning and she could barely walk. She felt so good that she just wanted to go to sleep. And she did just that after freshening up first. She smelled bacon cooking as she dozed off. She woke up a couple of hours later.

"Corey." She called out for him, but he didn't answer. She went downstairs and searched through the house for him and there was no sign of him. She went into the kitchen and found her plate and a note that he had left for her on the dinette table. *"Gotta make a run"*

She called him to tell him how much she appreciated him finishing the breakfast and taking care of her stress. He didn't answer. [*Not this again*].

****

Shauntel was sitting in the courtroom with her stomach doing all kinds of flips. On top of her nervousness about the court hearing the baby was kicking like it was trying to come out right on the court room floor. The baby had become really active every since she was two months pregnant. She was convinced that the baby was a future soccer player the way it kicked around all day. The stylist had done her thing again. Shauntel was looking all business in her black ruffle neck sleeveless dress with a gray blazer and gray leather pumps. Her hair was pulled up into a naturally curly ponytail with a bang in the back. She wore simple diamond stud earrings and very light makeup. She looked like she belonged on the cover of Forbes Magazine.

Nate was sporting a black suit with light pinstripes, a gray shirt with a white collar and a black and white tie. His shoes were black leather snakeskin with a silver buckle on the side.

Court was not in session yet and everyone was just waiting for all of the Attorneys to prepare their clients for the day's business. Attorney Hartford came over to where Shauntel and Nate were sitting. He shook both of their hands and told Shauntel to follow him. She followed him into a conference room where the two prosecutors on her case were already seated. Shauntel had a sudden urge to puke. She bolted from the room without one word hoping that she would make it to the bathroom in time. After she was done spilling all of her breakfast, she pulled herself together as best as she could and returned to the conference room shaking. Mr. Hartford seemed to be genuinely concerned about her. He ushered her into the corner of the room. "Are you okay? If not I can ask the judge for a continuance."

"I'm okay, just a little nervous. Why are we in here with the enemy?" Shauntel was whispering.

"Don't worry you are about to be pleasantly surprised." Attorney Hartford joined the prosecutors at the conference table and Shauntel followed suit.

The tall bony white man from Shauntel's original hearing had been joined by a lady assistant district attorney for the purpose of the trial. She was just on the verge of being fat with blonde stringy hair and pale skin. She looked like she never got enough sleep from the wrinkles and bags under her eyes and it was apparent that she drank too much coffee from the color of her teeth. She spoke first.

"Attorney Hartford, I take it that you want to make a plea offer?"

Attorney Hartford smirked at her confidently. "I take it that you take it wrong Ms. Clay."

The DA must have been offended. "That's District Attorney Clay to you."

Shauntel's attorney did not miss a beat. "I'm sure it is, District Attorney Clay. I am not here to make a plea offer. I am here to save you some time though."

The skinny man was getting impatient. "Would you just spit it out already Hartford?"

Attorney Hartford reached into his briefcase that was sitting on the desk and pulled out a small stack of papers. "Now that we are done with all of the pleasantries, I just wanted to give you both a heads up on the evidence that was just submitted to the judge." He handed each prosecutor a copy of a few documents. He continued.

"Awww, the beauty of technology. What you have before you is a copy of Ms. Barnes cellular phone records. If you look at the highlighted section you will see that on the day in question, Ms. Barnes used her cell phone to make a call right around the time that the fire department said the fire was started at her home."

Everyone was confused except Attorney Hartford. The man DA grew more impatient. "And your point?"

"If I could finish please! If you look at the last few pages of the documents I have given you, you will see that there is a record of each cell phone tower Ms. Barnes' cell phone hit and exactly at what time. I had her cellular provider to map it out for those who may not be able to understand the technical point. If you look you will see that the cell phone tower the call began at is the cell phone tower located right behind her fiancé's home and she was hitting that tower for quite a while. If you follow the trail you will see each tower she hit after that while on that same call maps out the route from her fiancé's house to her house. You will want to pay particular attention to the fact that her cell phone did not hit the tower nearest her home until after the fire department had been on scene for a while. This corroborates her initial statement to the police that her house was already on fire when she arrived."

The lady DA interrupted this time. "All that proves is that *somebody* used that phone on that day at that time, not that Ms. Barnes did."

"That's where you're wrong *District Attorney* Clay. The number that Ms. Barnes dialed that night was to a Ms. Tasha Thornton who vividly remembers the complete conversation of Ms. Barnes telling her she was on her way home to get some clothes and spend the night at her fiancé's house so that she would know to meet her at his house instead of at her home. She is an influential woman with a clean record who is ready to testify not only to that but also to the numerous incidents of stalking and terror that Ms. Barnes has endured over the last few months I also have Mr. Nathaniel Whittington ready to testify to the many stalking incidents and the fact that Shauntel's story is true. I won't even mention that my client is pregnant, hmmm a pregnant victim of a stalker. I'm sure the jury won't be sympathetic to that at all. And...... What do you have?"

Both DA's looked dumbfounded like they were searching for something to say but couldn't find the words.

So Attorney Hartford continued. "I would love to proceed with this trial just so that my client can be cleared of all charges. However, don't you think it would be an egregious waste of all of our time and the state's money? The only logical decision would be to drop the charges!"

The DA's looked at each other then back at Shauntel and her attorney. The male DA adjusted his tie. "Would you give us a minute?"

Attorney Hartford gave Shauntel a gentle reassuring tap on her back.

"Sure."

Shauntel and Jackson Hartford stepped out of the room so that the DA's could discuss their options. Shauntel breathed a huge sigh of relief as soon as she stepped into the hallway. Attorney Hartford was wearing a huge smile of victory. Shauntel had never seen him really smile before. She was so relieved that she embraced him like he was her recovered child who had been missing for years.

He was shocked by it, but he was more than pleased that he had again accomplished his goal of seeing his client go home free.

After a lengthy discussion, both DA's decided that it would make much more sense to drop the charges against Shauntel for now. They knew that if they went to trial with the lack of evidence they had, stacked against the evidence the defense had, she would be found not guilty. But if they dropped the charges now, they could always recharge her after they found more concrete evidence to charge her.

All parties shuffled back into the courtroom. As soon as Shauntel's case was called DA Clay told the judge that the state had decided to drop the charges due to some newly available evidence. The judge was looking at the graph of Shauntel's cell phone locations. She looked up and peered over her glasses like she had become famous for doing. She gleamed at the prosecutor like she was crazy and giggled a bit. "Well I would think so Prosecutor Clay. Shauntel Barnes all charges against you are dismissed without prejudice. You are free to go!" She banged her gavel.

****

After court Nate dropped Shauntel off at their new house they had purchased right before the wedding so that he could go meet up with Corey and discuss some business. She had decided to really start looking into the possibility of opening a restaurant business. She had already read up on the legal particulars of opening and running a restaurant. She had all of the necessary information to get her Management Food Handler's license. She had a few prospective locations that were being sold at very reasonable prices because of the recession. The only thing she needed to do now was call Mike so that he could get her connected to the right people for purchasing a business location and making sure that everything was up to code.

She grabbed her cell phone and dialed Mike's number. A woman answered the phone. "Hello?"

That caught her off guard and she wasn't sure what to say. "I must have dialed the wrong number."

The female's voice came through distressed. "Are you looking for Mike?"

"Actually I was."

"I'm sorry to tell you that Mike passed away yesterday."

"What?!!"

"Yes. I'm sorry but he lost his battle with cancer."

Shauntel tried to make sense out of what the lady was saying. It was just a little over a week ago that Mike had walked her down the aisle and gave her away at her wedding. She tried to think if he looked sick but her mind was too overloaded to focus.

The lady on the other end broke her thoughts. "His funeral is scheduled for next Saturday. I can have his secretary text you the particulars to this number if you want me to." All Shauntel could manage to say was, "Okay, thank you." The lady disconnected the call.

CHAPTER 14

Mike's funeral was held at the largest church in the area. The capacity was 6,000 people. Every seat was filled. There was an overflow room with a whole bunch of gigantic flat screens broadcasting the service. Shauntel was so glad that she and Nate had arrived an hour early or they would not have gotten a seat.

The funeral revealed so many things about Mike that she never knew. She found out how he had been abandoned by his parents as a child. He had basically raised himself from the time that he was a small boy. He never even knew if he had any siblings. He was a strong young man with a lot of charisma, working his way into the right circles despite his many stints in foster care homes and state run facilities. To know Mike was to love Mike. He made comrades in every arena you could imagine. He had friends in the criminal world, the education world and even the legal world. Despite his odds, he graduated from high school as Valedictorian with a full academic scholarship to any university of his choice. He went on to graduate from the University of Michigan Summa Cum Laude with a Masters in Business.

Fresh out of college, he started a number of successful businesses in Detroit. He never forgot where he came from and the people who were still hurting there.

The remarks part of the funeral went on for 2 and a half hours with dozens of people getting on the microphone testifying how Mike had turned their lives around. One man had lost his whole family to a drug addiction. Mike was the sole reason he had gotten clean and turned his life around. Another testimony came from a woman who had lost everything, including her husband, job, home and her children. Mike was the one who got her a job, bought her a house and paid her attorney fees so that she could get her children back from the state.

Until then Shauntel had never thought about how much she didn't know about Mike. She attributed it to the fact that he was always more interested in helping other people with their struggles than focusing on his own. The most important thing that she knew about him was that he had a pure heart.

The funeral lasted for almost five hours. It was truly a celebration of life. When the services ended, the family was escorted out first. Mike's wife looked at her eye to eye on her way out of the church. Even under the black veil Shauntel could tell that she was strikingly beautiful and extremely hurt over Mike's death.

****

It was the day after the funeral. Shauntel had just made it home from The Detroit River. She had gone there to collect her thoughts. When she made it to the porch she noticed that a package had been left there. She picked the package up and read the label and it was addressed to her. As soon as she entered the house her cell phone started ringing. She put the package down on the console table and answered the phone.

"Hello."

It was Tasha. "Hey girl."

"What's up Tasha?"

"I just had to call you and chew you out about keeping Corey a secret for so long."

"What are you talking about?"

"Girl, he is a stallion. Stella done got her groove back. I can barely walk and I mean that in a good way."

"Girl you are so nasty!"

"I know, right? But you are wrong for not introducing me to him earlier. I think I'm in lust!

Shauntel laughed. "You are crazy."

"How did court go?"

"It went wonderful. My attorney dug up my cell phone records and found that I was talking to you on the phone around the time the fire was set. The cell towers were able to prove that I was nowhere near the house when the fire started. They dropped the charges."

"I am so happy for you! You want to go to dinner later?"

"Sure. We can do that. This baby is making me want to eat everything in sight."

"Cool. Is eight good?"

"Perfect."

"See you then." They hung up.

Shauntel went and took a long hot shower and got comfortable in her lounging teddy. She poured herself a glass of

Sparkling Juice and sat on the couch to relax. She remembered she had a package. She grabbed the package and sat back down on the couch. She was trying to open the package but it was sealed extra tight. She was talking to herself. "Why would they seal this so tight? Is it that serious?" She had to search the house for something sharp enough to cut through the reinforced tape. She finally was able to find some razor blades that she had stashed in the back top of the bedroom closet. She went back to the living room and used the razor blade to cut through the tape. She pulled the flaps open and the last thing she remembered was the small explosion that knocked her to the floor causing her to lose consciousness.

****

Nate had thrown caution to the wind and decided that he was going to take care of Byron on his own so that all of the drama would be over. He just had to be strategic and not act off of his emotion because that is what always got people caught up and locked down. He didn't want his love for Shauntel to make him do a sloppy job that could come back and bite him in the ass. He shuffled up the block as quick as possible so he could meet Corey at the club and get an update on any information he may have gotten. He had to make the meeting brief because he had to go meet with the insurance adjuster afterwards to sign the paperwork to get his insurance check for the repairs to his company building. When he entered the club, he spotted Corey immediately. Evolution was empty with the exception of the two of them and a few employees who worked the day shift. Nate walked over and gave Corey some dap before taking a seat.

Corey was nursing a double shot of Jack Daniels. Nate was a little concerned. "Man you look a mess. What's up with that?"

"That's because I am a mess. Your girl has a brother worn out."

Nate inquired further. "Tasha?"

"Hell yeah. I thought Unique was a challenge but ole girl is like the energizer bunny for real."

They said in unison, "Keeps going and going and going and going." They laughed and gave each other some more dap.

Corey continued. "I thought she was going jump my bones in the middle of the restaurant after I had already been putting it down for almost 12 hours."

Nate encouraged him. "You just keep giving it to her like there's no tomorrow so we can get the information we need. Were you able to get any info yet?"

"Not yet. I was trying to make her comfortable with me first. I don't want to scare her off before she starts talking. I'm going to hook up with her tomorrow so I will start to chip away at the ice then."

Nate stood up. "Cool. I've got to head over to the insurance company so that I can handle this business to get these repairs started."

Corey downed his whiskey in one gulp. "That's good news because a brother needs to be working and making his paper!"

"I hear you. Don't worry though I've got your pay for all of the days we've been off. I charged it to the insurance."

"Good looking out."

Nate's police officer friend from school, Calvin walked up to the bar where Nate and Corey were sitting. He noticed Nate there.

"What's up Nate?"

"Too much! What's up with you Big Calvin?"

"Just stopping by to drop my girl's lunch off for her." Calvin had been dating the bar tender for about a year.

"Alright I gotta be out." He gave Corey and Calvin both dap and left the club. He was headed to the insurance company so that he could get his money and begin the repairs on his business. Then he planned to take a trip across town to prepare for a job he had hoped he would never have to do.

Before he could pull out of the parking lot, Calvin tapped on his passenger side window. He rolled down the window. "I don't mean to step into your business, but the last couple of times I've seen you, you've been stressed man. Is it something I might be able to help with?"

Nate thought about it. It might be a good idea to have a police officer on his side right now. "Get in."

Nate filled Calvin in on all of the stalking incidences, the charges Shauntel almost had to go to trial for because of it and the drama with Byron at the club. Calvin agreed to look into some things and see if he could help and get back with him.

****

Tasha had been calling Shauntel for the last two hours and she wasn't answering. She had called Nate and Corey a few times but neither of them answered either. She decided to drive over to the house to make sure everything was alright. When she pulled up in the driveway, an eerie feeling came over her. She shook it off and went to ring the doorbell. She stayed outside for about ten minutes knocking on the door and calling Shauntel's cell phone and house phone. She heard the house phone ringing but there was no sound of movement coming from inside. Tasha didn't know what to do or think as she sat in her car contemplating her next move. Her cell phone rang and she snatched it open without even thinking about looking at the caller ID. It was Nate. She told him about her concerns. He had not talked to Shauntel either. He had to cut his surveillance on Byron short to rush home to check on Shauntel. He had gathered enough information because he had been tailing Byron for the last few hours. He had even discovered where Byron lived and he was planning to take him out that night. Nate pulled up to the house a few minutes later and Tasha was still waiting in the driveway. He opened the door and there were very loud fumes in the air. He wasn't sure what it was but he told Tasha to wait outside and to leave the door open. He pulled out his gun and started to walk through the house to see if everything was okay. He searched the whole house and everything looked as if it was in order except for the empty package that lay in the middle of the living room floor with debris spread all around it. He stepped outside because the fumes were making him dizzy. He called Shauntel and her cell phone just rang. His heart sunk to his knees. He was mad at himself for not handling this situation by now. Because of his carelessness, the love of his life was missing and he didn't know if she was dead or alive. Then his anger turned to vengeance. He told Tasha to call the police to report Shauntel missing and wait in her car with the doors locked. He went inside and grabbed one of his guns and gave it to Tasha. "Anything that looks suspicious, point, aim and take it out!"

He walked to his truck. Tasha was confused. "Nate, where are you going?"

He looked at her like his life was over. "I'm going to find my wife!"

****

Shauntel woke up naked in a daze trying to figure out where she was. She was blindfolded, but she could tell that she was not at home. Her mouth was gagged and her hands were tied behind her back. The room was dimly lit and the bed she was in had an odd odor to it. She wiggled around in an attempt to get out of the bed. She made it to the edge and was able to scoot off of the bed. When she stood up she fell hard on the floor because she hadn't noticed that her legs were tied together. A masked man came running into the room she was in and just stared at her. She tried to speak but the gag in her mouth made her words inaudible. The man scooped her up in one motion and gently placed her back on the bed. He began to caress and kiss her face. She was so confused and wondered who this person was. She squirmed and made her protests known by squealing loudly. None of that seemed to deter the man. He continued to caress her body and moved south fast. He was caressing one of her breasts and sucking passionately on the other. She continued to squirm and squeal hoping that eventually her protests would make him stop. On top of being violated, she felt weird because this man's caress was actually making her aroused. He continued to go south with his hands and mouth continuing to make her juices flow down below. He untied her feet and rose to her sweet spot. He gobbled it up like he hadn't had anything to eat in years. Soon, Shauntel wasn't fighting it anymore because it just felt too damn good. Within minutes she was climaxing in this stranger's mouth. He sucked up all of her juices and proceeded to plant gentle kisses on her inner thighs. Shauntel was completely embarrassed. Then anger set in and she started kicking at him violently. He quickly hopped to his feet to avoid being kicked. She heard his footsteps leaving the room. A few seconds later, she heard him re-enter the room. Then she felt a needle prick in her arm and she quickly lost consciousness again.

****

Nate was flying through traffic once again determined to get to his destination and get Shauntel back. He sat in his car a few houses down from Byron's house and waited for his car to show up on the block. He didn't have to wait long. Byron pulled up a few minutes later. Nate casually walked toward Byron's house. He strategically made it to Byron's walkway at the same time that Byron did. He quickly pulled his gun out and pointed right at Byron's temple. "Do exactly what I say or I will blow your brains out right here all over this ground." He made Byron go into the house as he followed right behind him, never taking the gun from Byron's head. Once inside, he told him to lock the door and put on the handcuffs he'd gotten from the Eye earlier that day. Byron locked the door while Nate kept the gun trained on him. Byron turned around to face Nate and quickly ducked down and rushed Nate's legs slamming him to the floor. His gun went flying across the floor. Nate socked him in the face. But because of the position he was in, he wasn't able to get off a good hit. Byron was barely fazed by the punch. He jumped off of Nate and went for the gun. Nate was fast. He caught Byron by his legs and tripped him up. He slammed to the floor face first. They both got up and Byron was still trying to go for Nate's gun. Nate had more leverage this time as he ran up behind Byron and socked him hard with a right hook. Byron hit the ground again flat on his back. Nate retrieved his gun. He threw the handcuffs at Byron and waited for him to cuff himself. Then he ushered him into the kitchen and turned on the stove and all of the burners. The fear in Byron's eyes was evident. He pointed the gun directly at Byron's face. "I'm going try to make this easy for you. Tell me where Shauntel is right now or this is going to get really hard."

Byron was out of breath when he responded. "I don't know what you're talking about."

Nate was growing impatient. "So you want to make this hard?" He picked Byron up in one swift motion and slammed him down on the hot electrical stove burner. He put the gun closer to Byron's face. "You smell that? You're going to be dinner in a minute. Where the fuck is Shauntel?"

Byron was screaming and squirming. "I don't know where she is."

Nate's eyes turned bloodshot red. "Don't fucking playing with me!" He smacked Byron across the face with his gun and blood oozed out of his face.

Byron dropped his head and started sobbing. "Just kill me man. I swear I don't know where she is."

The kitchen was getting smoky and Nate didn't want to call any neighbors' attention to Byron's house from smoke fumes or smoke alarms going off. So he snatched him off of the stove and sat him down on a nearby chair. He grabbed a pitcher and filled it with water then doused Byron with it so the smoke would disappear. He told Byron, "We will get around to that. But you are going to tell me where she is first."

Nate grabbed a long sharp knife from the knife block that was sitting on the counter. "You can tell me now or this is going to really get painful." He picked Byron's leg up off of the chair and dug the knife into the back of the thigh making sure he hit the Sciatic nerve, something he had learned about back in middle school. Byron yelped in pain. Nate covered his mouth to mask his screams and dug the knife deeper into his flesh. He put his mouth up to Byron's ear. "I'm tired of playing with you homeboy. Tell me where she is or die right now." Byron shook his head in agony and tried to say, "I don't know." His words were inaudible.

Nate's phone rang and looked at the caller ID. It was Shauntel. He answered the phone quickly.

"Tel where are you?"

She was whispering. "I don't know. Somebody kidnapped me."

Shauntel paused. "I'm trying to listen. But I don't hear anything. Please get me out of here. Call the police or something. This man is crazy and I don't know   what   he   might   do   next."

        "What do you mean next? What did he do to you?"

He heard Shauntel sobbing. There were noises that sounded like a struggle and the call went dead. He tried to call her back at least 50 times, but her phone kept going straight to voicemail.

Nate stepped back, made sure his silencer was attached properly and shot Byron point blank in his head. Byron slumped over and took his last distressed breath. Nate ransacked his house looking for any clues that would lead him to where Shauntel was. He regretted killing Byron now, because there was nothing there to give him any clues. He just knew in his heart that Byron wasn't going to tell him what he wanted to know. Once he was sure that there was nothing there that could help him, he removed any trail of him being in the house and he left.

****

Nate hadn't slept in days. He was doing everything he could think of to find Shauntel. He was on his way to meet with The Eye to see if he had found out anything, because the police department didn't' seem to be doing anything valuable to find her. He had talked to the detective in charge many times over the last 5 days and he never had any new information. Nate was stressed out! He had to get some answers today. He opened the door to leave and the UPS man was walking up to his door. He handed Nate a package and asked him to sign for it. Nate did. He thought about the incident with Shauntel before he opened it. He looked it over and noticed that there was no return address. *'How do these delivery services just let people send packages without identifying themselves?'* He decided to open the package outside just in case it had any kind of explosive device or toxic chemicals in it like the package Shauntel had opened right before her kidnapping. The package was small, similar to the size of a business envelope. He opened it and noticed that there was an oversized card inside. It had a message on it that had been put together with letters that had been cut from a magazine. The big bold message read:

"GiVe HeR uP oR DiE! AnD I'm NoT ByRoN!"

****

This time when Shauntel woke up she looked around and noticed that she was in a seedy hotel. She was no longer blindfolded or chained up. She was free to move. There was nobody there but her. Her first urge was to search for her cell phone. She didn't know where it was though. She looked on the nightstand for the hotel phone so that she could call her cell phone and make it ring to find it. The hotel phone was gone.

Her instincts kicked in. She grabbed the nasty looking comforter off of the bed and wrapped it around her naked body. Then she took off running to the Hotel's front desk. When she got to the window, she pounded on it to get the clerk's attention. He had his back to her. He turned around looking bewildered. He appeared as if he had just had a fix.

"Help me! Call the police!"

The young white druggie threw his hand up. "Calm down. What happened?"

"Call the police. I was kidnapped!"

****

Once again Nate was at the hospital for Shauntel. This time, he was just there to pick her up. The doctors had examined her and found that she did not have any physical damage. The police had already taken Shauntel's statement. They informed Nate and Shauntel that the hotel didn't have any video cameras installed and the front desk clerk was so high that he didn't remember who had checked in or out during his shift. There were no other witnesses. They claimed to be following up and trying to find new leads. Nate knew it was all bullshit and they were not going to really try to find out who had kidnapped Shauntel. He was just happy that Shauntel and the baby were safe. He would take care of this on his own. They were both also relieved that they had finally started a paper trail of this crazed stalker because it would help Shauntel in the future if the district Attorney decided to try to charge her again.

CHAPTER 15

Tasha couldn't wait to touch base with Shauntel after all of the drama she had been through. She wanted her to know that she had her back no matter what. They had talked briefly but really hadn't had time to have a heart to heart. She also couldn't wait to get all the juicy details of the honeymoon. They had scheduled a girls' day out. Their day was starting with an appointment to get their hair done with their cosmetologist from high school, Ne-Ne. Ne-Ne was the kind of girl who had mad skills that most cosmetologists only dreamed of. One would think that she stepped out of the womb with a perm, blow dryer and flat iron. She really should have been doing hair amongst the stars, but on the contrary, she was a hoodrat and proud of it. She was proud of sleeping with married men and taking them for what they had. She was never seen without popping her gum and talking smack.

Shauntel saw Tasha out of the beauty salon window arriving fashionably late as usual. Her long flowing weave was blowing in the wind like she was standing in front of a diva fan. She had on black leather pants that hugged her body and a blue blouse with a plunging V-neck. Her jewelry was a white chunky bracelet and white necklace to match. Her shoes were pink red bottoms. Shauntel still didn't understand the concept of color blocking. But she wouldn't hate on it because Tasha looked fabulous. They greeted each other with a hug. Shauntel complimented Tasha on her look. "Girl you're wearing that outfit."

Tasha returned the favor. "And girl your glow is glowing."

Shauntel seemed as if she was trying to mask her gloom. "Thanks."

"Shauntel are you okay?"

She hesitated. "Yeah. I'm fine. My mind was just somewhere else. This baby is making it hard for me to focus."

Tasha tried to console her. "I am so sorry about what you went through. I'm ready to kill a mofo, real talk."

"Listen to you Little Ms. Gangsta. I really don't want to talk about it Tasha."

Sensing that the emotional wounds were still too fresh for Shauntel, Tasha dropped the subject.

They sat quietly in the lobby waiting to be called. Shauntel was curious about her friend's love life. She changed the subject. "So what's up with you and Corey?"

"That's a long story."

"Girl I've got all day. It's nice just to chill and get away from the drama of life."

"Well, I'm really feeling Corey."

"Really?"

"Yes. Why did you say it like that?"

"No reason. I just never thought you too would hit it off."

"That's the problem."

"What do you mean?"

Tasha lowered her voice. "I mean I don't know if he feels the same way. Honestly we're still just dating and on most days it's like were on the same page. Other days it's like he's a totally different person."

Shauntel tried to explain. "You know that he has been through a lot with Unique so that could be it. If not, we'll just chalk it up to him being a man." They shared a much-needed laugh.

"That's enough about me. Tell me about your honeymoon!!"

She was excited to tell Tasha about how awesome her honeymoon was. Shauntel didn't hesitate to give Tasha all the juicy details including how beautiful the ocean was and the many activities they had tried while there. Shauntel loved the water. No matter what was going on in her life, it always seemed to calm her. They went snorkeling, sailing, horseback riding and even took a helicopter tour. She told her about how nice the dining was. They had a full couple's day at the spa. She ended her long explanation. "Good thing I'm already pregnant. I have no doubt that if I wasn't I would have been at the end of that honeymoon, whew!"

Tasha and Shauntel were both under the dryer waiting for their 30 minutes to be up so that they could get their spots in the chair. Shauntel was reading vogue and intrigued by a story about a woman who had endured the unthinkable. Her husband had cheated on her and got his mistress pregnant at the same time that they were expecting their first child. Tasha was reading a psychology magazine as she had been doing for the past few months since her incident. Her therapist had told her that if she felt it was necessary to tell Shauntel about her past betrayal, it was totally up to her. Whatever she decided though, Dr. April had made it clear that she was there with her. She still had not told Shauntel her dirty secret because Shauntel had been so temperamental every since she found out that she was pregnant. But Tasha's conscience had been eating her up like a 300 lb. man who hadn't had a meal in months. The psychology magazine had an article in it about the naked truth. The premise of the article was that one was never completely free until they were completely honest with themselves and the important people in their lives. As usual, Tasha took this as a sign to be completely honest with Shauntel about her betrayal.

Tasha had fought with herself long enough about whether or not to tell Shauntel about the Junior situation. Considering the facts that junior was out on bail and Byron was dead, the recent stalker attack really helped her make the decision to come clean. She lifted her hair dryer hood and nudged Shauntel on her thigh. Shauntel looked over at her and lifted her dryer hood also. Tasha wasn't talking so Shauntel inquired about what the nudge was about.

"What's up Tasha?"

"Shauntel I have to tell you something and I hope that you don't get upset about it. I have wanted to tell you this for a while now, but I didn't want to jeopardize our friendship. First let me say that I am telling you this because I genuinely love you like a sister and I don't want there to ever be any secrets between us. I trust you with my life and I want you feel that you can do the same."

Shauntel looked at her confused. "Tasha you are scaring me. I hope that this is not more drama. I don't know how much more I can take."

Tasha leaned her head to the side and cleared her throat. "Shauntel you may look at it as drama, but I look at it as my personal growth. I hope that you can find it in your heart to understand and forgive me. I have a confession. I had some envious feelings toward you since twelfth grade when you went to the prom with Dominic until recently. I really liked him and when you went to prom with him, I felt like that was the ultimate form of disrespect. I never would have done that to you. Recently though, I have been able to work those feelings of jealousy out and fix what I had going on internally. Before I did though, I paid Junior to trash your place. I don't know what I was thinking. I couldn't have been in my right....."

"What the fuck?" Shauntel was upset and it showed in her voice and her body language.

"Hold on Shauntel, let me finish."

Shauntel stood up and was in Tasha face instantly. "Hold on my ass! You are finished! So all of this drama I've been going through with this stalker BS is all because of some crush you had in high school on some random nigga?"

"No. Wait Junior is not the one who has been doing the stalking...."

In a flash Shauntel had punched Tasha square in her face. She grabbed her by her hair and snatched her up out of the chair. "You dirty bitch! I thought you were my girl and you would put me through all of this!"

Tasha didn't want to hit Shauntel because she didn't want to hurt the baby. So instinctively, she grabbed Shauntel's hands and tried to pry them from her head. She was trying to explain, but before she could get a full sentence out, Shauntel had slammed her on the floor by her hair. Shauntel proceeded to stump Tasha wherever her feet landed yelling out obscenities the whole time. "You stupid trick!.... After all that I've done for you!..... You talking about we're sisters!... Bitch you ain't no sister of mine."

Tasha was trying her best to shield her face until she passed out and Shauntel noticed she wasn't moving anymore. Shauntel snapped out of her crazed trance and realized what she had just done. She fell to the floor on her knees and dropped her head into her hands and began to weep like a baby. All of the beauty shop staff and customers were standing there in awe. Ne-Ne was the only one to spring into action. She was used to hood drama. She ran over to Shauntel and snatched her off of the floor by her arm. "I don't know what kind of drama y'all got going on, but you need to get out of here before the police get here." Many of the beauty shop customers had already called 911. Shauntel was exasperated, but she was also exhausted from all of the drama. Her body felt like a dead weight resting on Ne-Ne. Ne-Ne knew that she had to bring Shauntel to her senses, so she shook her as hard as she could in an attempt to get her to understand. "Shauntel, the police are on their way. If you don't want to go down, you have to get out of here now!" Shauntel was starting to focus and understand the situation. She looked back at Tasha lying on the floor in her own blood unconscious and realized that she needed to make her escape. Her mind was telling her to go, but her legs wouldn't move. Ne-Ne shook her again but harder this time. Shauntel thought, *'this girl is cock-strong'*. Shauntel was finally able to force her legs to move. She rushed out of the shop, hopped into her car, started the car up and peeled out.

****

"Have a seat Shauntel." Shauntel looked at the beautiful not so comfortable looking sofa and sat down hesitantly. Looks were certainly deceiving in this case. It felt like she was sitting on millions of pillows. "I invited you over here so that we could have a serious discussion."

"How did you even know I exist? I have never met you."

"Oh, honey I know a lot more than you think I know."

Normally words like that would have made Shauntel uncomfortable coming from the wife of the man that she had once had an affair with. She wasn't sure if it was Mrs. Bradford's southern drawl or the calm in her voice that kept her from taking the words offensively. She continued. "Me and Mike didn't have a conventional marriage at all."

Shauntel squinted her eyes. "What do you mean?"

She chuckled a little bit. "Relax. We weren't swingers or nothing like that. We just had a different kind of love from most married couples. We were more like family than romantic husband and wife. I have known about you since Mike first met you."

Shauntel swallowed hard. "Really?"

"Yes ma'am."

"And you were okay with that?"

"Like I said me and Mike knew what we were to each other and we accepted that. See when I met Mike I was in a bad situation. To make a long story short, everything in my family went horribly wrong. So I packed up my stuff and left Georgia and came here to stay with this guy I had met online. I was only twenty-five years old and this guy took advantage on my naivety and self-esteem issues. Before I knew it I found myself on the streets selling my body. I had been working the streets for a few months and had recently started experimenting with cocaine to numb myself from what had become my life when one-day Mike pulled up to take care of some business on the street where I was working. I saw him and instantly knew that he had money and would be willing to pay generously. But I was new at the prostitute thing so I didn't even make eye contact with him. The other girls were all over him offering him any and all kinds of sex. He didn't seem fazed at all as he went gliding right by them turning them down tactfully."

Shauntel cut in with a smile. "That was Mike. He could tell you off nicer than anybody I've ever met."

"Yes he could and he was also very observant. When he came out from handling his business, he walked over to me and asked me what I was doing out on the streets. I told him that I wish I knew and that it was a long story. He asked me to take a ride with him and I did.

He took me to a little diner on the other side of town and when we walked in, he was like a celebrity. Everybody in the restaurant knew him. He was so humble though. He never came off arrogant. He looked at me and said "I'm listening." I just poured my soul out to him right there. I told him how my mother had died suddenly and my father had disappeared mentally and emotionally except for when he wanted to take out his anger on me physically. He started beating on me regularly for the smallest things. I missed my high school prom because I was too bruised from his beatings to go. My boyfriend who was my only friend was so hurt by me standing him up that he broke it off with me. I was so depressed that I basically became a hermit. The only time I came out of my room was to eat or go to the bathroom. I figured if my dad didn't see me, he wouldn't beat me up. My only outlet was my computer and I started chatting with this guy from here. We had what I thought was an instant connection. After a couple of months, he told me that he wanted to rescue me from my situation. He bought me a plane ticket and sent me some pocket change to have for my trip. That was the first form of affection I'd had since my mother had died." She was tearing up and shaking her head back and forth.

"Mrs. Bradford, I'm so sorry you had to go through that."

"I was too at first, but everything happens for a reason. And if I hadn't gone through this I would have never met Mike. I would go through it again a thousand times if it meant I got to meet him every time. Excuse me for a minute." Mrs. Bradford was choking up a little. She got up to get some Kleenex and came right back.

"I told him how I got caught up with this guy and how he used my vulnerability against me. He knew that I didn't know anybody here and didn't know anything about Detroit. I was stuck. He told me I was going to sale my body or else. I had jumped out of the skillet into the fire. The beatings my father had been giving me were nothing compared to the beatings I was getting from him. Anytime I went against what he wanted, he would beat the hell out of me. Mike sat there and patiently waited for me to finish my life story. Then he asked me 'do you want to be on the streets?' I looked him dead in his eyes and told him I would do anything to not be! He told me that he would check on me in a week and if I was still serious, he would make that happen for me. Mike was charming but I thought he was just talking. He drove me back to my post and gave me $550. He told me to find someplace to hide $500 of it. Since $50 was my normal fee, my pimp wouldn't get suspicious. Sure enough, a week later Mike pulled up at the same time of day. He walked up to me and said, "You still want to get off the street?" I figured nothing could be worse than the situation I was already in. I looked at him like he was crazy and told him I wanted to be off more than I did the week before. He told me to get in the car and the rest was history. He helped me get off of cocaine, cleaned me up, put me up in one of his houses and put me through school. He even talked to my former pimp and convinced him to never bother me again or else. Eventually I told him about my dreams and he helped me make them come true. He was impressed with my abilities in project management. The hotel was my idea and I helped him bring it to reality. Of course he paid for everything but I was the brains behind it. He moved me into his house shortly after that and made 'an honest women' out of me, as he would say."

She paused and smiled gently.

Shauntel added, "That sounds just like him."

"See I knew that Mike loved me, but he wasn't in love with me. I'm sure you know that his motto was honesty and truth and that's exactly what we had, a love that was based on honesty. He didn't believe in sugar coating things or keeping secrets from each other and he let me know that he was in love with you."

"He did?"

"Yep. Mike stayed with me because he felt obligated to me not because he was madly in love with me and I was woman enough to accept that. He was well off when we met, but the hotels made him extremely wealthy. I also think that he felt that it would completely crush me to have the one man who I genuinely loved to leave me. He also had promised early in our relationship that he would never leave me. He never wanted to break a promise. I thought about leaving him many times just so that he could be totally happy with you, but I also felt obligated to him. He saved my life after all and I never wanted to hurt him by being disloyal. So we stayed together all of these years."

Shauntel didn't know what to say. "Wow Mrs. Bradford, that is really deep."

"And it gets deeper." She opened the drawer on the cocktail table, pulled out an envelope and handed it to Shauntel. "He left this for you just in case he didn't make it. Mike knew he was sick for a long time. He knew his chances to beat the cancer were very slim.

You know that he was always prepared for everything."

Shauntel took the envelope and held it in her trembling hands. It simply read "Curves". That had been his nickname for her the entire time they had known each other.

"Shauntel you don't have to read it now if you don't want to. I know I just laid a lot on you. I'm sure this is not the most comfortable setting for you. But I want you to know that I have no hard feelings toward you. We were both lucky enough to be loved by the greatest man to ever grace this planet."

"No, it's ok. I'll read it now." She opened the envelope and pulled the letter out.

Hey Curves. Of course I'm no longer living if you're reading this. I want you to know that I love you more than anybody else in the world. I guess mama was right when she said if you love something let it go and if it comes back to you then it's yours forever. If it doesn't, then it was never meant to be. I let you go in that life and God didn't see fit for you to come back to me before he called me home. I guess it wasn't meant to be in that life. I do believe though that it will be meant to be in this life and I look forward to your return on this side. Curves, I know that the baby that you're carrying is mine. I felt it in my soul when I first found out that you were pregnant. I promised you that I would continue to spoil you even after my death. I want you to know that I intend to take care of you and our daughter or son. I know that you will be a great mother. I only have one request. Please teach our child to live by the same principles that I lived by, honesty. Tell him or her that daddy loves them and that I am so sorry that I wasn't able to be there. Live your life to the fullest because tomorrow is not promised. I will always love you and don't you ever forget it.

Truth,

Mike

Tears were streaming down Shauntel's face. She was overwhelmed. Mrs. Bradford reached back into the table drawer. She pulled out a check and handed it to Shauntel. It was written for $200,000,000 to the order of Shauntel Whittington. Shauntel was sobbing and slowly shaking her head up and down. "Mrs. Bradford, this can't be right."

"Sweetie, it can't be more right. I have one identical to it. Take that money and take care of yourself and your baby. I feel like we are family. I love everything that my husband loved and he more than loved you. If you ever need anything, know that I am here for you. And by the way, call me Pam."

CHAPTER16

Shauntel was finally able to sit down and write out her Thank You cards for her wedding gifts and attendees. They were extremely late because of all of the drama between the kidnapping, Tasha's betrayal and Mike's funeral. She was finally bouncing back from the trauma of the kidnapping. Nate had been unbelievably supportive of her. She was blissfully in love with him and just knew that he was her soul mate sent straight from God. She was debating whether or not she should send Tasha a card for such a wonderful job with planning the wedding. She thought about Tasha's betrayal and wondered should she let that take away from her trying to make things right by making her wedding day so special when her cell phone rang Monica's "Why I love you so much". She knew it was Nate and she answered in her most sexy voice. "You miss me already?" He didn't respond. She greeted him again. "Nate?" There was still no answer. "Can you hear me, Nate?" She could hear a conversation between two guys in the background, but it was muffled. Worriedly, she pushed her ear into the phone so that she could hear the background better. She realized that he had dialed her without knowing that he did. She could hear Nate talking, but he wasn't talking to her. "This is all my fault!"

She heard the other voice answer and wasn't sure who it was but it sounded like Corey. "This ain't your fault dawg. You already handled your part of it. Don't let it mess you up in the head. You have to stay focused. I'm finally at a point where I can get Tasha to talk. You've moved into a new place that nobody knows about and it's fully protected. Calm down. Everything is going to be okay."

"If I hadn't paid old dude to scare Shauntel into my arms, I would not have had to force him to move to another state and be paying for his babysitter to make sure he doesn't come back this way. On top of that, if she hadn't cut all of those dudes off all at once, I wouldn't be sitting here trying to figure out who the hell is terrorizing her. The bad part is that I can't be sure that old dude out of state isn't having somebody else here to do his dirty work. This crazy mofo kidnapped and raped my wife, there's no telling what he might do next!"

Shauntel was flabbergasted. She couldn't believe that the same man she was just fantasizing about being her soul mate would stoop so low to put her safety in danger just to make her his. She quickly hung up the phone. She was too disgusted to listen to anymore of the conversation. Tears began to flow involuntarily. She was shaking and confused as she tried to comprehend what just happened. She stood up and paced the floor and unsuccessfully attempted to wipe her tears away. She had nobody to turn to. Her best friend had betrayed her. The love of her life had committed an unforgivable sin. Her protector, Mike was dead and her rock, her grandmother was dead and gone too. Just then, she thought about what her grandmother would do in her situation. She fell to her knees and cried out to God. "Lord why is this happening to me? Is there anybody in this world that I can trust? I try to give my all to people, but I keep coming up with the short end of the stick. It seems that you are the only one I can depend on. Please tell me what to do!" She begged between sobs and tried her best to wipe her tears away. They wouldn't stop falling.

She laid her face on the carpet and prayed silently. She heard a still voice come from inside of her. *"You have a new friend in Pam."* She looked around to see where the voice had come from. Nobody was there but her. She heeded God's advice. She grabbed her cell phone so that she could call Mike's wife; except, she never locked in her phone number. She got up and packed an overnight bag as fast as possible, got in her car and headed to Pam's house.

****

Shauntel was apprehensive about ringing the bell at the gate of Pam's oversized mansion. She felt guilty for being in love with Pam's husband even after his death. She shook her head back and forth and put the car in reverse. She heard the same still voice from inside her. *"Ring the bell."* She didn't waste time this time trying to figure out where the voice was coming from. She knew that it was the spirit of God. She put the car back in drive and nervously rung the buzzer. She heard the sweet voice of what sounded like an angel. "May I help you?"

"It's Shauntel. I'm here for Pam. Pam is that you?"

The voice came through just as sweet as before. "Yes it's me."

Shauntel began to try to explain. "You told me that if I ever needed anything...."

The gate buzzed and opened. She exhaled loudly and pulled into the winding driveway. She parked her car adjacent to the front door. Pam stood in the door in her white boy shorts, white tank top and white athletic sandals with a welcoming expression on her face. Shauntel's fears dissipated as she got out of the car and went in the house. Pam gave her a hug, closed the door and walked through the foyer to the family room with Shauntel in tow. "Come on in."

Shauntel was so shook on her last visit that she hadn't noticed the splendid beauty of the house. This time she actually noticed the shiny hard wood floors surrounding the two enormous staircases leading to the upper level that reminded her of the movie Scarface. She looked up and marveled at the huge sky window that illuminated the whole area. As she entered the family room, Pam motioned for her to take a seat. She did.

Pam looked at her with concern not wanting to delve right in. "Please excuse the way I'm dressed. I just came back from my daily run and haven't had time to shower and change."

Shauntel shook her head in agreement.

Pam's next question was full of empathy. "Are you okay?"

Shauntel hesitated. "I'm not sure."

Pam's expression exhibited that she was thinking before responding. "Do you want to talk about it?"

Shauntel's words just fell out. "My new husband has done the unthinkable. My best friend betrayed me. I have nobody to turn to because my only family, my grandma, she....she died and Mike. Mike, he died too and I'm all alone. I'm sorry for burdening you with all of this, but I don't have anybody else." She dropped her head in her hands and burst into tears.

Pam chose her words carefully. "Shauntel there is no need to apologize. I meant what I said when I told you that if you needed anything that I would be here for you. One thing I learned during my reformation is that no matter who leaves us, God will never leave us! Now let's take a deep breath and talk about one thing at a time. You said that your husband did the unthinkable. What did he do?"

Shauntel took the deep breath as Pam had suggested and began to tell her everything. She told her about how she had been being stalked and was kidnapped. She also told her that she had recently found out that Tasha had paid someone to break in and vandalize her house. She enlightened Pam on how her and her grandmother had taken Tasha in and was the only real family Tasha had known since her mother died. She made sure to add a description of the strong woman she'd known her grandmother to be. She also told her about the conversation she had overheard between Nate and Corey.

Pam listened to the whole story intently. "Shauntel, it sounds like the people you love and trust the most have let you down."

Shauntel looked at her like she was crazy. "That is an understatement."

"Maybe it is. The fact is that God will not put more us than we can bare. He doesn't allow us to go through anything without a reason."

That convinced Shauntel that Pam was a few cards short of a full deck. "What in the world would be the reason for him allowing me to be betrayed on every important side?"

"That's a question that I don't have an answer for, but I'm sure He will reveal it to you soon enough. I'll give you an example. When I went through what I went through on the streets, it was the lowest point of my life. I would have given anything to get a do over in life. I woke up many days asking God and myself how I had ended up in that situation. But there was a reason for me going through those things. It wasn't until years later that I realized that I had a responsibility to help girls out who are at that same low point. I started an organization to help girls get off of the street. It has been really successful and fulfilling. So even though I hated going through it, I would do it all over again in order to get the satisfaction of knowing that I can help change other women's lives for the better."

In some strange way, Pam was starting to make sense to Shauntel. She still couldn't see how her being let down the way she had been would benefit her or anybody else though. But she did believe that God knew better than her and for now she would allow him to work. She was still hurt and pissed off at Nate and didn't know what her next move should be.

"So am I just supposed to overlook all of the wrongs that people have done to me?"

"Not overlook them per se. Just know that God says that vengeance is His and that people reap what they sow. Some people call it Karma."

"Now you sound like my grandma for real."

Pam told her in her granny voice, "Please chile, I ain't that old." They both fell out laughing. Shauntel started to reminisce about her grandmother and all of the great advice she used to give her. At the time she was too young to understand what her grandmother meant. But life had a way of making old lessons resurface and make perfect sense.

Pam interrupted her thoughts. "Are you hungry?"

"I guess I could eat something."

"I have an idea. Mike told me that you were an excellent cook. How about we make dinner together?"

They made their way into the kitchen and cooked a full soul food meal. They made honey baked ham, dressing, collard greens, macaroni and cheese, candied yams and sweet potato pie. They worked well together and talked about everything from Mike to fashion. Pam turned out to be really cool. Shauntel was glad that she had made the decision to come see her. They even shed a few tears; Pam because Mike wasn't there to eat the huge dinner they had prepared and Shauntel because Pam's tears made her reminisce of all of the good times her and Mike had shared over the years.

Pam packed most of the food up so that she could take it to the shelter. Then they sat down and ate the little bit she had set aside for them. Shauntel wondered how Pam was able to eat that kind of food and keep her athletic figure. She had the body of a sixteen-year old athlete. After they were done eating, Pam gave Shauntel a tour of the house and showed her to one of the guest rooms and told her that she was welcome to stay as long as she needed to.

****

Shauntel was covered in blood as she stood in the middle of a circle of corpses. She looked down at the machete in her hand and it was covered in blood too. She wondered how and why the people were dead. She looked around and tried to comprehend where she was. A huge man that resembled a giant walked up to her and she could feel his disappointment in the air. He peered into her eyes and she felt it all the way to her soul. He was hurt by what she had done. She had killed those people. She tried her best to tell him how sorry she was but no words would come out. He turned his back to her. She ran around him to apologize to his face. She wanted him to know how sorry she was for what she had done. Every time she ran around to face him, he would turn his back to her. This went on for a long time. Then there was a loud rumbling and the ground shook. She had to work hard not to lose her balance and fall. As soon as she steadied herself, she felt the rumbling again. Somebody called her name. She got excited because he was going to hear her out. She heard her name again but the man's mouth wasn't moving. "Shauntel!!!" She looked up from her bed and noticed she had been dreaming. Pam was standing in the bedroom door talking to her. "Forgive and ye shall be forgiven."

She was confused as to what Pam was talking about. "What did you say?"

Pam repeated herself. "I said I have to make some runs. Call me on my cell if you need me."

"Okay."

Pam left the room. Shauntel was trying to pull her thoughts together. She realized the voice she heard say "Forgive and ye shall be forgiven" was not Pam's voice. It was the same voice she had heard from the inside of her the day she had come to Pam's house. It had been three days since she arrived at Pam's house. She was not taking any of Nate's calls other than the one she took to curse him out about being such a selfish asshole. He had tried with all of his might to beg her for forgiveness and explain his point of view. She was not having any of it! She told him that their marriage was a fraud and she didn't want anything to do with him ever again. The dream she'd just had and the voice had her rethinking that decision.

She got out of bed and started to gather some clothes for the day. She took a shower and got dressed. The whole time she was fighting with herself about the forgiveness statement and the dream. She finally gave in to the voice and decided that she was going to start the forgiveness process by going to see Tasha so that they could talk about their issues. She had to start forgiving the people who had wronged her so that she could have peace and forgiveness.

On her way out of Pam's house, her cell phone rang. Her ringtone let her know that it was Tasha. She felt that was confirmation that she was doing the right thing. She answered the call.

"Hello."

"Shauntel I know that you probably don't want to talk to me right now. But I'm begging you not to hang up on me. I really need you right now. Can you please meet me at my house?"

"It's funny that you asked me that because I was actually on my way to your house to talk to you about some things."

Tasha exhaled. She didn't know what to say. She never imagined it would be so easy to get Shauntel to come over.

"Tasha?"

"Okay. I'll see you in a little while."

Tasha disconnected the call and stared down the barrel of the gun that the stalker had pointed at her face. She prayed that God and Shauntel would forgive her for leading Shauntel back into the hands of the stalker and that the stalker wouldn't kill her even though she had done what he demanded. As she finished her prayer, he told her, "good job". Then he punched her in the face. She hit the floor unconscious.

Shauntel drove to Tasha's house. When she knocked on the door, it opened a bit. She walked in and called out. "Tasha?" When she stepped into the living room, what she saw made her gasp. Corey was standing over Tasha with a bloody bat. Tasha was lying in a pool of blood. He turned around and looked at Shauntel and smiled broadly. "My angel. I knew you would wake up and realize that I'm the one for you."

Shauntel was confused. She hated that she had left the gun Nate gave her in her car. "Huh?"

He motioned for her to come to him. "I knew one day you would see that Nate was not good enough for you. I am so happy that we're finally going to be together. Shauntel I love you so much. You are the only woman for me. I never thought that I would get you. But, here you are. Come and give me a hug."

She looked around him to see if Tasha was okay. "What did you do to her?"

"She's fine. I need you to know that I was the one to spot you first the night you and Nate met. He stopped me before I could approach you. He came and talked to you instead. But I knew the second I laid eyes on you that you were the one for me."

A creepy chill ran over Shauntel. "Corey what are you talking about?"

His voice turned demanding. "Get over here so I can show you!"

She didn't know if she should try to run out of the door or talk some sense into this obviously mad man. She tried to buy some time to think. "Wait a minute Corey. I'm married to your best friend. How is this supposed to work?"

"You tell that nigga the truth! We are in love and there's nothing he can do about. He'll just have to get over it. If not, I'll help him get over it."

She was still trying to think of what her next move was going to be. "Is that what you did to Tasha? You helped her get over it?"

Corey moved fast and before Shauntel knew it, he had his hand around her neck. She was struggling to breathe. He had her pinned against the wall. Then he started kissing her roughly. She was still pinned to the wall and struggling for air. She noticed that his lips were the same lips of the kidnapper's. Her thoughts were going crazy as she thought back to the surveillance camera recordings the day Nate's condo had the manure left on the lawn. Corey's frame matched the silhouette they saw. The night that someone was shooting at Nate, the body that hopped the fence also matched that same build. Hindsight was definitely 20/20. Corey was also the only other person who had handled Nate's key ring that had the key to her house on it.

He finally eased the grip on her neck and stopped kissing her. She gasped for air. Tasha stirred and moaned. He snatched Shauntel by her wrist and started to drag her. She snatched away from him. "Let me go!"

His eyes instantly turned red. He reached way back and backhanded her knocking her to the floor. She was unconscious. He went and started small fires in every part of the house. On his way upstairs, he kicked Tasha in the ribs again. First he lit small fires in every room upstairs. Then he lit fires in every room downstairs. He bent down to pick Shauntel up to leave. Before he could get a good grip on her, Nate had hit him hard across his temple with his nickel-plated 9 mm. Corey and his bat fell back on the floor. He started laughing. "You punk motherfucker. You know that you only got Shauntel by default and she is rightfully mine." He stood up wiping blood from his forehead.

Nate couldn't believe his ears. "You are a sick twisted bastard."

Corey continued his ranting. "Naw man you a selfish bastard!" He picked up his bat. "I guess I'm going to have to help you get over it." He went to swing the bat at Nate. In mid swing the bullet from Nate's gun pierced his chest and he flew backward.

Nate knew he had to hurry and get Shauntel and Tasha out of there because the smoke from the fires was getting thick. He saw Calvin at the door. "You grab her," he told Calvin pointing to Tasha. He scooped Shauntel up in one swift motion and the two men carried both women out to safety.

Calvin had been investigating the whole situation every since he had run into Nate at Club Evolution. He started by looking into the backgrounds of everyone who was close to Nate and Shauntel. He had discovered that Corey had spent some time in a mental institution before because he had Possessive Personality Disorder. As long as he took his medication he was fine. Whenever he didn't take it, he could be really dangerous. Consequently, Calvin had installed a listening device in Tasha's house. Not to mention, Nate had told him that Tasha hired Junior to vandalize Shauntel's house. He figured he would kill two birds with one stone. Earlier he'd heard the conversation between Corey and Tasha. During Corey's ranting at Tasha, he'd confessed that he had been the stalker all along. That prompted Calvin to quickly get Nate on the phone and fill him in on the details while they both made their way to Tasha's house.

Now they stood outside making sure that they had their stories straight at the same time giving the fire enough time to brew to make sure that Corey wouldn't make it out alive before they called 911. Shauntel had regained consciousness. She was really worried about Tasha's injuries. "We need to call 911 or she is going to die!"

Calvin tried to convince her. "Nothing we do now is going to hurt or help her. We just need a few more minutes."

Shauntel was determined. "Yawl better call 911 now or I am!"

Calvin countered her. "Do you want to have this psycho stalking you for the rest of your life?"

Shauntel thought about it for a few seconds. "No. But we have all of the evidence we need to prove that he is a crazy stalker who tried to kill Tasha and assaulted me. Nate shot him in self-defense."

"That may be true but do you really deserve to have to go to court for that asshole's trial after all that he put you through?"

Nate interrupted their debate talking on his cell phone. "Yeah 911, I need an ambulance and the police immediately!"

Nate knew how much Tasha meant to Shauntel and he didn't want to risk her life just to satisfy his own personal satisfaction that Corey was dead or to protect himself from prosecution for shooting Corey.

****

Tasha had been in the hospital for a week. Shauntel had not missed a day of visiting her. She was still in a coma. The doctor's were giving her a 50/50 chance of survival. She had two broken ribs, a concussion, a collapsed lung and a closed head injury.

The beating had caused internal bleeding and she had hemorrhaged and lost a lot of blood. The hospital staff had to give her five blood transfusions since the day of her arrival. They would not be sure what the effects of her closed head injury would be until she finally woke up from the coma.

Shauntel lovingly brushed Tasha's hair and talked to her for encouragement.

"Tasha we have been through a lot together. Through it all, we've always had each other's backs. You are too strong to let this beat you, too strong to let that psycho beat you. Other than Nate and this one in my stomach...." She rubbed her belly. "You're all I've got. You have to pull through this. Who else is going to be an auntie to this little soccer player? I just want you to know that I forgive you for everything and I hope that you can find it in your heart to forgive me for hurting you. I'll be right here when you wake up."

Nate walked in. "Hey baby, you ready?"

She looked up at him thinking about how much she loved him and how she had almost let go of the man that God had made for her. The police had ruled Corey's death self-defense and cleared Nate of all charges.

"Yes I'm ready." She bent down and kissed Tasha on the forehead. "See you tomorrow."

The next couple of weeks were touch and go for Tasha. Every now and again her vital signs would become irregular. The hospital staff did everything they could to regulate them. Her ribs were healing successfully, she no longer had a concussion and her blood count had remained normal for the past two weeks. Their only concerns were what the consequences of the closed head injury would be.

Shauntel had arrived at the hospital early that Thursday. She was determined to be there when Tasha woke up. She wanted her to feel like she had somebody in the world who still loved her. She wasn't sure if Tasha could hear her or not. But she made it a point to read the Bible to Tasha everyday and tell her of all of the progress she had made with the planning of the restaurant business. She also told Tasha how much she needed her so that they could be successful together.

She did her daily routine. She washed Tasha up and brushed her hair. Then she pulled the visitor's chair up to the bed and held Tasha's hand while reading her scriptures from the Bible.

"The L<small>ORD</small> is my shepherd; I shall not want.

He maketh me to lie down in green pastures: he leadeth me beside the still waters.

He restoreth my soul: he leadeth me in the paths of righteousness for his name's sake.

Yea, though I walk through the valley of the shadow of death, I will fear no evil: for thou art with me; thy rod and thy staff they comfort me....."

Tasha squeezed Shauntel's hand. She stopped reading and looked up. Tasha's eyes were open. She couldn't control her eyes though; they were kind of rolling around in her head. Shauntel ran to get the nurse on duty. The nurse called for the attending physician. They all quickly made their way back into the hospital room. The doctor grabbed Tasha's hand. "If you can hear me, squeeze my hand." Tasha squeezed his hand.

The doctor asked her a series of questions and told her that if the answer was yes to squeeze his hand and if it was no to do nothing.

"Is your name Tasha?" She squeezed.

"Do you know how you got here?" Nothing.

"Do you know how old you are?" She squeezed.

"Are you in any pain?" Nothing.

Tasha was squirming and trying to speak but nothing was coming out.

"Do you have something to say?" She squeezed.

The doctor got her a pen and pad. She struggled to write but finally got her thoughts down. She turned the pad around for Shauntel to see. It read, "Thank You."

Epilogue

It was opening day of Shauntel's restaurant. She had put her blood, sweat, and tears into the creation of it. It was all paying off today. She and Nate stood at the red tape. Nate held his baby boy, Nation who looked like his twin in his left arm with Shauntel holding onto his right arm. Pam stood facing them with the tape cutting scissors in her hand. Tasha stood behind them for support. It had been a very long journey for her over the last year. She had basically had to learn how to do everything again as if she were a child. She had to learn to talk, walk, eat and most other common things. She had come a very long way and still had quite a ways to go. For the most part she was back to normal with the exception of a limp and an occasional breakdown. The breakdowns would occur when she was overwhelmed. It causes her to stutter and not be able to complete a sentence until she rests for a few hours in the dark. Despite all of her challenges she had assisted Shauntel in making the restaurant beautiful. There was a crowd of people behind them filled with celebrities both local and National.

Pam looked at Nate and Shauntel. "I can't tell you how proud I am of the two of you. God is definitely smiling on you now that you have decided to accept his perfect path for your lives. I wish you much success in all that you do. Without further ado, welcome to Soulfood Nation!" Pam cut the tape and the celebration began.

The festivities went well into the night and little Nation was sound asleep on top of a table in his baby carrier. The four of them stood there admiring him. Nate hugged and kissed Shauntel affectionately. The crowd applauded. He looked at her intently. "You sure make a beautiful baby."

"So do you."

"I have an idea. Let's go to Paris."

"Nate we can't take Nation to Paris."

Pam jumped in. "I'll keep him."

Shauntel was still worried. "What about the restaurant? We just opened."

Tasha chimed in next. "I can take care of it while you're gone."

Pam followed. "And I'll help her whenever she needs me."

Shauntel smiled ear to ear. "You all are too good to me."

They shared a group hug.

Don't forget to cultivate your dream while working your reality!
~Alexis Brown

Excerpt from **Karma Returns – The Sequel**
(available soon)

"Oh yeah baby girl I see it. I see those chills, you all shaky. Craving a hit?"

She was squirming as she sat on the floor with her legs crossed Indian style. She attempted to blow her hair out of her eye through the small part of the gag that had come loose.

"Does it hurt?"

> She shook her head no, "Unh-uh." She had her arms folded so tight that the handcuffs were bruising her thighs. She rocked back and forth nervously.

"Why are you sweating baby girl?"

She bent forward and moaned loudly from the pain.

He pulled the small plastic packet from his pocket and waved it back and forth.

She tried to bury her face in her chest. Barely audible through the gag she was wearing came, "Please no. Just let me go."

He snatched her head back by her hair. He was snarling and foaming at the mouth. "Bitch, let you go? Did I let you go last time? You forgot who I am! I'm DADDY and don't you ever forget that. I did not giv e you permission to leave. Do you know what that's called?"

She didn't answer.

He snatched the gag off then slapped her hard. "Do you hoe?"

She shook her head no. She knew she'd better do what he said right now. She had seen this look in his eyes just before he put one of the other girls in the Intensive Care Unit at Receiving Hospital.

"That's called a runaway slave. You is Masa's property! Now you owe me for all of the monetary transactions I missed out on from that sweet ass for all those years."

She was desperate. She knew she needed to get to an AA meeting and get some medication to help with her withdrawals. She mumbled. "I can pay you for it."

"Naw you gonna honor our original agreement." I had that ass promised to a lot of people out here. Then you let that punk ass Mike come along and ruin everything including my reputation. Had me looking weak in these streets!

She really wanted to scream how weak she really thought he was, but she knew better. He had the upper hand at the present moment and she was gonna have to bite her tongue.

"You gonna be my example of what happens when you cross Silky!"

She was getting a cramp in her neck from how he was holding it back. She squeezed her eyes closed tight to take focus off of the pain. He bit the pack open and held the small plastic baggie up to her nostrils. "You want it don't you bitch?"

Pam was sobbing hysterically until she heard his belt jingle and realized she didn't feel the plastic anymore.

She had to focus. She did not want to get another beating like the one she got from the biting incident.

As she looked up through tears, she saw him pulling his little dick out. He sat it on her forehead. Pam's breathing was really rapid. As much as she tried, she was not able to calm it.

"Why are you shaking Pamela?" He pulled her hair tighter. The pain was intense. She finally gave in. Her words were almost clear this time, "Okay, Okay."

He crushed the coke and poured it in her nose. She sniffed it but before she could even enjoy its feeling, he took it to another level.

"Remix Bitch!" She felt liquid running. He was pissing on her face.

S ista girl,

You are so much more than your pretty face,
So much more than those panties with the lace.
So much more than your hips and lips,
So much more than your cookie and tits.
What you have to offer
Is much more subtle and softer.
Your grace, your style
And that beautiful smile;
That connects directly to your heart.
Your strength, your loyalty and smarts
Makes me recognize your beauty within
And know that you'd be priceless to any real man!
So don't allow him to exploit you
Instead make him dote on you.
Demand that he understands
The treasure that you are,
The pleasure that's so far
But worth the ride
Because when he arrives
The prize is inside!

Yours Truly,
~*Sista Girl*

Alexis Brown   *Karma Burns*

Alexis Brown is on her way to becoming a Best Selling Author of her coveted urban mystery Karma Burns. Alexis' first love has always been the written word. Over the years, she has obtained expertise in a variety of areas with studies in psychology & information technology. She has an array of poems she presents via spoken word at local events. She is also a ghostwriter of several well-known titles. Her online talk show, The Salad Bar that is currently taping where she provides a platform for up and coming entrepreneurs to spread the word about their businesses while encouraging her audience with healthy living and weight loss tips. Alexis now resides in the Triangle area of North Carolina where she enjoys cooking, listening to music and traveling to destinations where she can peacefully sit beachside with a pen and a pad. Alexis is currently finalizing the highly anticipated sequel to Karma Burns, Karma Returns. She is slated to release three other novels over the next year including Betrayal, Obsessive Compulsions and a Self-Help Book.

For Bookings, Email: aprilrosepromotions@gmail.com

Visit our website and sign up for updates, events and information: www.authoralexisbrown.wix.com/lexy

Made in the USA
Columbia, SC
14 April 2023